This is a work of fiction. Similarities to real people, places, or events are entirely coincidental.

SECOND CHANCE DANCE A DICKENS HOLIDAY ROMANCE

First edition. November 18, 2024.

Copyright © 2024 Bonnie Edwards.

ISBN: 978-1989226247

Written by Bonnie Edwards.

Table of Contents

What readers are saying about Bonnie Edwards' Dickens Holiday Romances...

Second Chance Dance: LET DICKENS WORK ITS MAGIC "...a beautiful, heartfelt story of love, loss, and new beginnings. I loved the chemistry between Nick and Laurel," 5 Star Amazon Review

The Winterland Waltz: Just like watching a holiday Hallmark movie

"For anyone who likes Hallmark rom-coms, this is a lovely simple romance of two people recovering from past mistakes." 3 Star Amazon Review

The Rumball Rumba: I absolutely love this book and series

"a beautiful and poignant story that I couldn't put down..." 5 Star BookBub review

The Tinsel Tango:

Simply Sweet "This is such a cute Hallmark style Christmas tale. The town is adorable..." 4 Star Amazon Review

Second Chance Dance
A Dickens Holiday Romance
Book 27
By
Bonnie Edwards

This book is dedicated to my dad who loved cars. Thank you
for making me the car buff I am today.
And to my mom, who made me the parent I am today.
(They turned out great, Mom)
And to my Nan who proved that happy endings can happen
throughout life. (even at 84)
And for Ted, always.

Chapter One

Rock Bay Casino Hotel - 50 miles from Dickens

Rock Bay Casino Hotel - 50 miles from Dickens Dutiful, boring, predictable grandmother Laurel Tabor stepped into the elevator, leaving behind her group of lady friends from her condominium building. To a person they loved the slots, and because she was a bore, she hated gambling. Or at least that's what she told herself. She'd let them convince her that this time, the weekend trip would be different, that she'd have fun.

She was still waiting for the fun to start, and she'd already been here two days, faking it.

Predictably, she'd had no fun. At all. Dutifully, she'd already called Trix, her daughter, to say she was on the way to her room. Boringly, that's where she intended to go.

Until he stepped into the elevator.

A man. Handsome, about sixty give or take, a head taller than her. Finally, something interesting happened. She leaned against the back wall of the car to give him room. Before she could study his face, he turned and tapped the button for the lobby.

She let her eyes and her mind wander. She fancied she'd be the perfect height to nuzzle his neck. Maybe lick his ear. Taken with her wild musings, she forgot to ask him to tap the button for her floor and ended up riding down to the lobby, where he got off without another glance her way.

Unpredictably, and with a quiver of excitement, she followed him. Actually walked a pace behind him on his left as he crossed the marble floored lobby and headed toward the bar. He drew to a halt at the entrance and glanced at her, then looked again.

He turned, giving her a full view of his face. Oh, mama, he was handsome. Square jaw, freshly shaven, kind deep brown eyes, and a friendly expression.

"I'm here for a quiet drink before I turn in. Care to join me? I'm on a road trip alone and haven't had a soul to talk to today." His voice sounded like silk on gravel and sent a new kind of quiver down her spine. Up close he appealed to her more than he had in the elevator.

"I'm on a weekend trip with friends, but I'm not much for gambling. I'm here for a quiet drink, too." Okay, she made the bold new decision as his words washed over her. As his eyes took in her figure, quickly and shyly. Why not be less predictable for a change? Less boring? She smiled at the man and hoped the fun was about to find her. "I'm Laurel, and yes, I'll join you," she said.

"I'm Nick. Nice to meet you, Laurel." His gaze settled on her smile, which made it widen. Oh, my. Things were about to get interesting.

Four hours later, she scooped up her panties, shoved them in her jeans pocket, scrabbled to grab her far-flung shoes and bolted out the door of his room, strangely exhilarated at her daring. Nick had left their nest of warm, rumpled sheets for a quick shower, so she didn't have a lot of time to make her getaway.

What had she been thinking? A stranger, in a strange town, strange hotel. That she'd chosen this man, in this place, for her first and only one night stand stymied her. But she could put wild and enticing and sexy in the column of her life titled *character description*.

As it opened, the heavy door handle clicked loudly in the quiet, but with the water running, Nick wouldn't hear it. She hadn't told him her room number or that she lived only fifty miles away. Come to think of it, he hadn't said what town he was moving to, either.

Good, neither of them could surprise the other and do something weird, like ask for more time together.

At fifty-seven, she'd had her first wild moment, her first rebellion against *staid and predictable*. The idea flummoxed her. But along with her shock, she now had a memory of having been, for once, a scandalous woman. She slapped her palm over her mouth to hold back a nervous giggle as she slipped into the hall. She'd never worn pants without panties on, never carried her shoes as she tiptoed down a hotel hallway, never felt the wonder she'd felt with Nick.

Not even with her husband, Keith, nearly forty years ago.

Never been so afraid of the feelings that she'd had as she and Nick shared a connection that spanned the emotional, intellectual, and physical. Two hours chatting in the bar, nursing her drink to keep her head on straight, and still, she'd come with him to his room to continue their conversation in comfort. She'd kicked off her shoes, folded her feet to the side of the sofa and he'd touched her cheek. She never should've tilted into his palm, never should've leaned in to test his lips, never should've fallen into the precipice with him.

But she had. And she loved it.

Nights like this weren't for women like her. Feelings like this weren't for well-behaved, dutiful grandmothers. But, oh! She celebrated these hours with Nick.

And now, she could go home to Dickens and keep her secret forever. If anyone noticed her secret smiles occasionally, she'd never tell them what they meant. No one would ever know that Laurel Tabor had had the best night of her life after decades of sleeping alone.

DICKENS – EARLY AFTERNOON

Nick St. James held the door open to Dorrit's Diner for his date. She preceded him in a swirl of floral perfume. He preferred citrus based scents but asking a woman what kind of fragrance she wore seemed picky when he got a hit on a dating site. Picky and a bit creepy. She stopped immediately on entering and he had no choice but to crowd behind her as she chose a table.

As she'd explained on the phone, by one fifteen the lunch crowd had been served and people had left booths open for newcomers. He hadn't lived in Dickens long enough to understand the rhythm of the place, so he'd bowed to her familiarity with the restaurant.

"There's a booth near the back that's been cleared," he said, hoping she'd move forward and take the perfume with her before he sneezed.

"That's fine." She headed for the booth. A slight gasp and movement in his peripheral vision caught his attention and he looked toward the counter.

It was *her.*

Laurel. The woman he'd wanted to find for two weeks. Having no leads, he'd officially given up yesterday when he'd called *Laverne? Shirley?* To arrange this coffee date.

Jeeze, Nick, get your act together. You knew her name five minutes ago. But at first sight of Laurel his brain seized on her and no one else.

As he watched, Laurel dropped something and sank beneath the top of the counter, out of view. But he was certain it was her. When she didn't pop back up, he became suspicious. To get a better look he'd need to lean across the counter. He took a step toward doing just that when he realized she'd hidden from him. He needed no more confirmation that the woman was Laurel, and he hadn't imagined her.

So much for what they'd shared. He should've understood she'd got what she wanted when he found her gone halfway to morning. But what about what he wanted?

Which was simple.

He wanted to get to know her. Laurel. *If* that was her name. Maybe she'd lied to avoid awkward contact afterward. He didn't know the protocol around one-night stands, but clearly, she did.

Her hiding on sight was his first clue that it hadn't been embarrassment that had made her run. He thought he'd assured her that she had nothing to be ashamed of, but when he'd found her gone—well—he'd drawn his own wrong conclusion.

His date settled in the booth and looked expectantly at him. Two women. The one he wanted, hiding from him, the one he'd brought, waiting with hope in her eyes.

Decent men didn't let things like this happen, he thought with a guilty glance toward *Betty? Veronica?* He sighed and continued to chastise himself as he moved toward the woman who wanted to spent time with him, as opposed to the one who didn't.

A simple coffee date: an initial meeting to see if they wanted to meet again. He could get through it and walk out of here without a word to Laurel, which is exactly what she seemed to want.

No biggie, they'd slept together, and she'd abandoned him when he'd left the bed to shower, despite having said she'd see him again. He'd get over it. Or he would have if he hadn't walked in here and seen her.

Still, he had to get through this date first, and without asking to move it to another restaurant.

LAUREL HEARD NICK MOVE away toward the booth in the back. The blood returned to her face. She could tell because her cheeks flamed hot. She took a slow breath in and then out as she listened to the small talk Nick made with his date.

Of all the coffee shops and diners in the state, why pick Dorrit's? What was karma up to, sending the one man she never wanted to see again to her place of work? And why had she agreed to handle the lunch rush alone today? She couldn't pass off Nick's table to anyone else.

She'd have to serve them. Walk over there as if nothing had happened with the man. Like she hadn't let him pick her up in a hotel bar and agreed—eventually—to go to his room. The plan had been to continue their conversation, but one thing led to the wrong thing and, well, they'd been human. A good woman would feel shame, but not her, no. Embarrassment made her dive like a tween behind the counter in Dorrit's Diner.

He'd brought a date in here! A stab of jealousy surprised her. She had no right to feel jealous. She'd been the one to sneak out. *Grow up. Act your age.*

She sucked in her belly to help her spine keep her upright. She wasn't a coward, she told herself. And this was her job.

She could do this. She could serve her first and only one-night stand. *Ever.* She'd handle this just like she did any other awkward customer, with calm, professional, detachment.

At fifty-seven a woman shouldn't have to slide to the floor in mortification over a simple one-time error in judgment. Those mistakes belonged to the young, not to grandmothers!

She rose to stand, but for the life of her she couldn't help a look over to where Nick sat. Small mercies. He faced the back wall and his date, a woman she'd seen in here before with other men. She had her answer then. It wasn't karma that brought Nick in here, it was the woman's habit to bring dates here after the lunch rush.

Again, she sucked in her belly, reached for the coffee carafe and two mugs for their table. Luckily, she knew the woman preferred her coffee with cream and no sugar.

If her brain let her speak, she'd mention that she'd memorized the woman's order.

Nick would have to tell her what he wanted. She hoped he wouldn't use the tone of voice that had turned her legs to jelly.

As long as he didn't say it was her he wanted, Laurel could get through this.

Chapter Two

L aurel swung past their table, her hips steady as she balanced two full plates on one arm and held a pot of coffee in the other hand. Laurel moving smoothly, efficiently, was a joy to watch. Nick couldn't take his eyes off her, watching for any sign that she recognized him. Unfortunately, he'd sat facing the wrong direction which meant his head was on a swivel.

Maybe her refusal to glance his way was enough. Maybe that was her tell. He grinned when he realized the truth. She did remember him and had no choice but to pretend otherwise. Her nametag assured him she hadn't lied about her name that night. At least something about their time together was real. He'd started to wonder if he'd dreamt it.

"The server knew your coffee preference," he said to the woman across from him. "Do you come here often?"

She'd driven over from the next county to meet him here.

"I've been three or four times. I like the town common and the interesting shops. Trim-A-Tree is great for Christmas gifts." A shift in her gaze said she wasn't being completely honest. But on a first date, who was?

"And no one knows you here," he offered with a nod. "I get it. Being seen on a date can be awkward. Gossip and all."

She flushed and nodded. "It's easier if tongues don't wag."

"I moved to Dickens a couple weeks ago. This is my first time in this place." His head swivelled as Laurel chuckled at something a guy at the end of the counter said. "Great little diner. It seems to have been here for years, so that must mean the food's decent."

The woman nodded and gazed somewhere over his left shoulder, disengaged, clearly hunting for another topic. While she thought, he turned his head enough to catch a glimpse of Laurel in his peripheral vision.

Average height, light brown hair tied in a jaunty ponytail that stuck out of the back of a vibrant pink ball cap, Laurel wore a smile that could stop traffic. She turned toward them, and he straightened. He didn't want her to catch him staring. Her smile fell away.

Guilt drilled through him as he tried to pull his mind back to his date, but the woman had begun to chat about reality shows that revolved around roses and young people on dates. He scrubbed his hand lightly down his face to order his thoughts and be more present. The woman deserved more attention than he'd given her.

Laurel walked past again, chuckling from some comment she'd heard at the far end of the counter. His ears perked up at her light laugh. The sound was throaty, mysterious, and sexy. And he remembered it well. It had been her laugh that night that had enticed him to ask her to join him in his room. It had been an innocent invitation. A desire to learn more about her, nothing more. Her laugh had made him want to spend more time with her after she'd taken two hours to finish her drink.

They'd been in an elevator together. They'd shared a polite smile and he'd seen a glimmer of humor and hope in her eyes as they'd stood at the entrance to the lobby bar. He'd offered to treat her to a drink.

She'd hesitated and he figured he'd struck out. But then she'd shrugged and agreed the night was still young.

A giggle from across his table drew him back to *Lucy? Ethel? Whatever.* He had to get Laurel out of his head, at least long enough to remember this woman's name. She giggled again, and he had to wonder what woman over fifty giggled like a young teen.

This one. Maybe her nerves had gotten the better of her.

Her profile on the dating app had made her seem more interesting than she was. No surprise there, he'd seen it before. Heck, maybe he'd fudged a bit himself.

Were they two phoney people going through the motions? Likely, he decided.

Cathy! That was it. Relief eased through him.

He waited for Cathy to take a breath.

"I enjoy rescue shows," he blurted. "The firefighters are my favorite." She hadn't asked, but he wanted to at least pay lip service to engaging.

"It seems to me those shows are for boys looking for heroes." She tapped the back of his hand. "And you don't seem at all like a little boy, Nick." One side of her mouth ticked up.

"Thanks." He gave her the smile she seemed to expect while wishing Laurel sat across from him.

This was useless. Maybe the next guy would fall for the flutter of eyelashes and the obvious shift of her body to draw attention to her assets. As he thought it, she crossed her arms under her breasts.

Maybe the next guy, but not him.

"Look, I'm sure you're a wonderful woman, Cathy, but—"

Her features hardened and she pulled back against the banquette. "And I'm sure you see yourself as a nice guy, but the way you ogle the waitress tells me you're a player. I don't have time for men like you. Good luck," she said brusquely and grabbed her purse. As she slid out of her seat, her cloying perfume wafted past his nose.

Nick frowned. He wasn't a player, and he didn't ogle women, but he could see why Cathy thought he might be ogling Laurel.

It wasn't as if he could confess that he'd spent half the night with their server in his hotel room.

If he were honest, that's what galled the most. He'd had *half* the night with Laurel, a few short hours, before she'd vanished like fog in the morning sun.

He had to get her to talk to him. Knowing why she'd run out on him seemed important and he'd never figure it out himself.

There was no rush, of course, because he lived in Dickens now. In a townhouse just off this square, in fact. He planned to be here for a good, long time.

LATER...

Laurel stared at her reflection in her bathroom mirror and stuck out her tongue. After the woman with Nick had stormed out, Laurel had disappeared into the kitchen. Not surprisingly, Nick left shortly after. He also left a generous tip with three words on the bill.

'No harm done.'

Was he being kind? Forgiving her for running out? He'd made it plain that night that he wanted to see more of her. He'd said as much when he'd got up to shower. But her bravado had run out and she'd told herself that she should never see him again.

The man was dangerous to her frame of mind. She'd liked him so much! His smile caught at her heart, his eyes had been warm, his tone by turns caring, slyly funny, and sexy. A younger woman might mistake a reaction like hers to be love at first sight.

But a grandmother knew better. A woman who'd lost the love of her life in her twenties didn't believe in fairy tales or happy endings.

A woman who'd raised her daughter alone while grappling with crippling grief had to be conscientious, diligent, devoted, faithful, to accommodate her child. Happy endings were for other people.

Up until that night with Nick, every word that came to mind described her; the way she lived, the way she *wanted* to live. But Nick had detonated all her best intentions. They'd scattered to the winds and when she emerged from the devastation, she'd run away.

Cowardly? Yes. Safe? Yes. And safety seemed far better for her than being brave in the face of her feelings for the man. And now, he'd come to Dickens and ruined her peace of mind.

Just like that.

No sooner had she convinced herself that she could let go of her self-blame for her out-of-character decisions that night and move on, than he'd walked into Dorrit's.

She'd spent hours chastising herself for her behavior since she'd scurried out of his room at three a.m. No matter that he made her feel like a woman again. That he made her feel wanted. He also made her wonder if her years of safe choices meant she'd missed too much of life.

A fifty-seven-year-old grandmother should not wonder what she'd missed. It was unseemly.

She'd been a grandmother for almost a year, but this thrum of yearning had begun months before her grandson had made his appearance. It had started in the dead of night when she'd woken alone and wondered what came next for her.

The yearning had churned into discontent. She hadn't told anyone how she ached. No one would understand. Every other woman she knew had their act together.

Heck, some of the widows in the building were happy to be alone.

Jack's birth last Christmas should have ended the dissatisfaction, but oddly, earning the moniker grandmother had only strengthened it.

Kind of late for a midlife crisis, but what else could it be?

She lifted a brush to her hair but halfway through the first stroke she stopped. Stared again at her face. Her lined, motherly face.

Motherly. The sour thought enhanced her self-pity, and she didn't care. *Matron. Crone. Grandmother.* The last word slithered into her mind. When had she settled into all the synonyms for old woman?

What had possessed her to accept Nick's invitation to his room? His considerable charm had worked, that's what. More, she'd reveled in it.

If she wanted company for the movies, she could ask Peter Jones to join her He came in regularly to sit at the counter. He was nice to look at, had a great smile, and a better sense of humor. There wasn't a day that went by where she didn't enjoy a genuine laugh with that man.

But flirt? No way. She hadn't flirted in years until she'd bumped into Nick St. James.

As a young woman, she'd had more attention than she'd wanted, but these days she was anything but an object of desire. Which made not flirting much easier.

Twenty minutes later, Laurel pulled a tray of buns out of the oven. Her kitchen smelled heavenly. Just in time. Normally, she'd be pleased with the batch, but she took no pleasure in the repetitive chore. Not anymore. She swiped an errant curl out of her eye, sighed, and moved into the bathroom to finish getting ready for the family dinner at her mother's.

It would be the last small family dinner of the year. In a couple of weeks, her sister and brother-in-law would arrive, and her nieces and their husbands would be at her mom's house more often. Both nieces and her daughter had married in the last three years. Life had settled and everyone else seemed happy.

She should be grateful for the wonderful things that had come to fruit. Determined to bring gratitude into her attitude, she headed out for her mother's place. They'd be planning for the Christmas season tonight.

They had a lot to plan for, especially at the Dickens Art Studio and Market, where Laurel spent half her working hours helping her daughter run the place. Trix needed her more than ever and Laurel enjoyed the time she spent there.

Working extra hours would help take her mind off Nick St. James; she was sure of it.

Chapter Three

"Some days I still can't believe I'm a great-grandmother," Laurel's mother said as she gazed lovingly into the crib at the sleeping baby.

"How did you feel when you were a grandmother for the first time?" Laurel had never asked before because the question seemed to have only one obvious answer.

Her mom smiled in nostalgic joy. "Deliriously happy. I still had your dad to enjoy it with. Life was good and had panned out beautifully."

"You didn't feel old or that there wasn't much future for you as a woman?" She bit her lip at revealing so much.

"What is this about?" Her mom turned and eyed her. "This isn't like you, Laurel. You've always been a stalwart woman, practical, not prone to fanciful questions about life. Do you feel okay?"

She shrugged and used a bland expression. "Looking at Jack I realize I have less time ahead of me than behind me, and I wonder if my practicality means I let some things in life slide by. Maybe I should have—I don't know—looked for more for myself? I might not be alone if I had." She shouldn't have said a word, but in the hushed nursery with only a sleeping baby to witness the conversation, she felt safe and open.

Her mother's expression turned to dismay. "Oh, Laurel. It's not too late to do something just for you." Her arm came up and settled on Laurel's shoulder. A hug and then a kiss on her forehead proved a mother's love was always needed.

"But?" she asked because she understood there must be a but in there, even if it was left unsaid.

"That's for you to figure out. Travel sounds good and there's a group in your building that arranges holidays. I've been invited. We could go together. A bus trip." Her brows knit in a frown. "Maybe."

"They focus on gambling and look for casinos. Not my thing." She'd never go again. Last time she'd joined them, she'd met Nick St. James and scared herself half to death with how much she loved her time in his arms. No way would she share this with her mom.

Mom would tell Jennifer, who'd tell her daughters who'd tell Trix. She'd have a lot of heartfelt concern to navigate, and she'd hate it.

She wasn't the family drama queen. No. She was responsible and dependable.

Boring, predictable and...lonely.

"Then a man," her mother said with a conspiratorial tone. "There are some good ones around, you know. I've heard of good results from some specialized apps. There are apps for every type of person. Young, old, queer, straight."

"Dating apps seem desperate." But she didn't know that for certain. She'd simply assumed.

"I've known more than one couple who found each other that way. But apparently there are a lot of frogs to kiss before you find your prince."

"I refuse to kiss frogs." Not after kissing Nick. Had she stumbled on a prince and not recognized him?

"Well then, like I said, it's for you to figure out. But whatever the right thing is, don't let fear stop you. Go for it."

Nick had actively changed things for himself while she dithered. He'd been happy to talk with her that night. They'd been completely engaged with each other. She'd never have thought herself capable of such a connection. Not at her age. Not when she'd been alone for decades. She knew he'd been happily married and lost his wife. He mourned for two years and then he'd begun online dating. He'd changed his life with that decision.

Her childish sprint out of his room may have doused a spark before it caught. She'd run away and then, to make matters worse, behaved like an overwrought teenager at Dorrit's.

Nick shouldn't have been in that hotel at all. What were the odds that they'd cross paths that way? She had no clue about things like that. About what made two people gravitate toward each other and take comfort from a stranger in a shallow encounter.

A voice near her heart spoke up. *There was nothing* shallow *about what she'd felt in his arms.* Ruthless, she shut the voice down as she ran over what she'd learned about him that night.

He'd told her he was moving to a small town to be closer to his grandchildren. He'd driven from Florida, and too tired to continue, had stopped for the night at the hotel. He thought the casino would be entertaining but gave up when the noise had become too much. He'd been after a quiet table in the bar when they'd ended up sharing the elevator.

She never should've let her imagine run wild as they'd ridden to the lobby. Nonsensical thoughts had invaded her mind, but she'd been powerless to stop them.

She knew in the morning, he'd continue his journey north, as she'd be on a bus with other women heading northwest, away from the coast. Their paths would never cross again.

Which was what she wanted. Until he'd shown up in Dickens.

The woman he was with at Dorrit's had come to the diner on several dates prior and Laurel assumed Nick had followed her suggestion to meet there. It wasn't like he lived in Dickens because he'd said he was headed north in the morning. When she'd scrambled out of his room, she thought she'd never see Nick St. James again.

After her ridiculous behavior at the diner, she was now sure of it.

"You look sad, sweetie. What's got you down?"

"Nothing, Mom," she said softly. "Just my own foolishness."

NICK PULLED HIS MUSTANG into a parking space in front of the Dickens Art Studio and Market, a huge red barn that had found new life in the last year. His former son-in-law, Jon, had married the woman who owned it after renovating the building to house her new business.

Meeting Trix had come at the right time for Jon, and he'd jumped on the chance to be a husband again. A father again.

And that new relationship had been the catalyst for Nick to reconsider his future. It hadn't been easy, but he'd started dating again. Not lucky enough to meet a woman the old-fashioned way, he'd signed up for online dating.

His first few dates had soured him on the whole scheme, but then, on the drive up from Florida, he'd booked a room in a hotel and walked across that lobby beside Laurel, and everything changed.

After she'd sneaked out of his room, he'd wracked his brain to figure out what had gone wrong when everything between them had seemed so right. Their shared humor, shared values, shared attraction. He'd tried to recall a way to track her down, but she hadn't said where she lived.

Then, two weeks later, having lost hope he'd ever see her again, he'd walked into Dorrit's diner on a first date. A bolt of attraction hit him for a familiar server who wore a jaunty pink cap and a smile that danced in her eyes.

In the week since he'd been to the diner, he'd thought a million times about returning to see Laurel, but he'd fought the pull. He was too interested, too attracted, to mess things up by being pushy or tongue-tied. He needed to settle into life in Dickens and plan a way to approach her so she wouldn't run again.

Deep in his soul, he understood that their one-night stand inexplicably worked against him. He'd spent a week coming to that conclusion, but the more the considered it, the further entrenched the idea became.

He wished that night hadn't happened because they could start fresh. He had a feeling that with Laurel, one misstep could blow everything to smithereens.

The only time in his life he'd felt this cautious was when he'd met his Jeanie. He'd used a slow and steady advance with her, and he could do it again with Laurel.

He climbed out of his car to find the late November air brisk. The wind picked up and golden leaves scooted across the pavement. They gathered at the base of the red clapboard. Mother Nature had given the nearly new barn a cheery golden foundation. Glad to be out of the chill, he stepped into the building and stood in shock at what he found there.

It was her again. Laurel. How odd that lightning would strike three times. Must be a sign. This time she wore snug jeans, suede ankle boots and a red fleece vest. She looked great with her light brown hair down in soft waves that rested atop her shoulders. She had threads of silver at her temples, which made it seem like Mother Nature had given her the gift of tinsel in her hair.

Her smile caught him again. The woman could light up a room. He took his time drinking in the sight of her because she hadn't seen him yet.

She chatted with one of the many vendors in the market, a man, early fifties, who sported a bun and wore a tie-dyed sweatshirt. It was Saturday and the place was hopping with customers. Most carried paper or cloth bags of merchandise. Could be early Christmas shoppers. *Christmas?* He'd almost forgotten it was nearly here. He hung back, pulled his scattered thoughts into line. Without Jeanie for the last couple of years, the holiday had barely made an impact. A couple of calls to his grandchildren to catch up with their news had been the extent of his celebrations. Going to a potluck dinner for singles in his retirement complex didn't count as a real Christmas dinner.

After a moment of earnest conversation and broad smiles, the man with the bun in his hair returned to his stall. His hand-written sign had a misplaced apostrophe, but it was clear he made and sold soaps and household cleansers that promised they were made from vegetable extracts.

When Laurel looked up, their eyes caught and held across the aisle of shoppers. His belly contracted but couldn't contain the nerves that jumped. He was done for.

He took a first step, followed by a second and a third, each one faster than the last, until he stood directly in front of her.

"Laurel," he said, looking into her azure eyes. Brilliant blue irises emphasized by thick black lashes. No wonder nerves leapt in his gut. "You can't hide this time," he said, trying for a teasing note.

"No, not this time," she replied softly, but her gaze darted as if she were looking for a secret door for another escape. "What are you doing here?"

"I came to meet my son-in-law's new wife but now, I'd rather spend my time talking with you." He wasn't sure where the words had come from except that he meant each one. *Step lightly.*

"Do you mean to say that you were on your way to Dickens that night? You never said where you were moving to."

"You never said where you live, either."

"For two people who talked for hours, we didn't say much that proved useful."

"On the contrary, I believe we said a lot of the most important things."

Her cheeks bloomed a spring rose color, and he warmed with hope that she understood what was behind his comment.

"I, um, have things to see to here. I'm helping my daughter get organized for the holiday rush." She checked her phone. "My lunch break is in an hour. If you have time we can talk then. Unless you get caught up with your family, of course. Meeting folks for the first time can go either way." She smiled encouragement. "I remember you mentioned your son-in-law had remarried after your daughter passed."

"That's right. Truth be told, I'm a bit nervous that his new wife will find it odd that I've moved here. I've been slow to reach out, but today's the day."

"I'm sure everything will work out."

He nodded. "I'll come find you after I meet her." He'd start his campaign by giving Laurel a chance to get used to him being around. "No rush."

"Good," she said softly. "That's good. No rush." But her cheeks grew darker red, so he leaned back to give her room. "Who is it that you need to meet? I can take you to them."

"Her name is Trix Warden, and she owns this building. Jon tells me she's here most mornings with their little guy, Jack. You must know her." The last was said because as he'd spoken her beautiful eyes had widened in shock.

"I know Trix better than anyone else in the world. She's my daughter."

LAUREL STOOD TRANSFIXED. Nick St. James had said they were extended family. They shared a son-in-law! But how?

Surprise molded his next words. "Well, small world. Jon's first wife was my daughter, Melody."

She raised her hands to her mouth to hide her gaping shock. "I'm sorry you lost her."

"I know. We talked about her that night."

"Of course. We did," she agreed. He'd shared his pain at losing his only child. She also knew his wife never moved on from the shattering loss. "Jon's a good man," she added, "and still speaks of Melody." Of course he did. Melody was Blair and Ben's mom, and they needed to share their family stories and history. She reached out and set her palm against Nick's forearm in a gesture meant to comfort.

Big mistake. His arm was as muscled as she remembered, and at the reminder of their physical attraction, sudden shyness overcame her. She fought it back. This was no time to act like a teenager. She dropped her hand.

"He is a good man," Nick agreed. "When they got married young and under less-than-ideal circumstances, we weren't as"—he searched for a word— "enthusiastic as we could've been. For years I've regretted my first reaction to their news about a teen pregnancy, but Jon and I made our peace a long time ago. He's one of the finest husbands a woman could have."

"He reminds me of my husband in a lot of ways. Both steadfast." And typical of the Nick she'd met that night. The man had an innate kindness that appealed to her on many levels.

"I remember you telling me about your husband. Keith, right?"

Her nod felt stiff. They'd shared so much about the big events in their lives, but next to nothing about the little details. She felt slightly ill at the reminder of how attracted they'd been to each other. The physicality of it. But she couldn't say that.

"We talked a lot, didn't we?" About so many things that mattered. She supposed it had felt safe to talk to a stranger, but afterward, when it became obvious they could have much more than a brief encounter, she'd cut and run. Like a coward.

He nodded. "We're blocking the flow of foot traffic." Shoppers sidestepped them on both sides of the wide center aisle. "Here I thought we'd chat later, and I've been taking up your valuable time. Other people need your attention." His words broke the spell of intimacy between them, and she nodded.

Tilting her head, grateful for the change of topic, she indicated the staircase at the far end of the barn. "Well, Nick, you can find Trix up in the office." She motioned to direct his attention to a wooden staircase that rose to a loft office. "I'll tell her you're coming. Knock softly because Jack could still be napping." She raised her phone and sent a text. "I'll come up and get you when I'm heading off for lunch. There's a food truck on the far side of the barn. Frank's hot dogs are great, but his smokies are better."

"I'd like that." His warm, kind eyes shone, and she recognized the same pull she'd felt that night three weeks ago.

"Go meet my daughter and my grandson," she said with pride. "Jack's a cutie."

Chapter Four

Nick settled across from Laurel at a picnic bench on the lawn beside the barn. They had their choice of tables because the air had turned colder, and they were the only customers staying outside to eat. He didn't mind because the tip of her nose had turned an adorable shade of dark pink. "You're okay? Warm enough? Your cheeks are pink."

She patted them. "I'm not sure it's just the cold that's making me blush." She groaned as if she'd spoken out of turn. Then she held up her hot dog. "I'll be better when I eat. I skipped breakfast because I slept in."

Her segue made him chuckle on the inside. "You can use my jacket if you get cold." He raised his own hot dog for a bite while she glanced away to some place he couldn't follow. Likely memories.

When she looked back at him, a shimmer of damp appeared in her eyes. The cold could do that. Offering his jacket couldn't.

"You okay?" he asked for the second time.

She nodded around a bite of her bun. After she chewed and swallowed, she responded. "Your chivalry recommends you. My husband did that sort of thing and it's been years since I was the recipient."

"I get it." He'd had a moment earlier. "When you asked what I like on my dogs, I flashed on Jeanie loading them up for me at family barbecues. A long marriage meant she didn't have to ask, and I appreciated that you wanted to know."

She frowned. "You asked if I'm okay. I'm not sure I am. It's awkward for me to think about that night. I don't understand the rules around what we did."

"Eff the rules." He took another bite. "I'm prepared to say that the night in the hotel never happened if that makes this easier for you."

Her lips parted and a long breath escaped as she considered his offer. Then she leaned so far over the table toward him that he thought she'd land on the top. "Fair enough. Eff the rules. It's been so long for me that they've likely changed anyway." Her wide grin lightened her features as she looked delighted. "I never saw you before you walked into Dorrit's on a first date. By the way, I could tell it didn't go well."

He chuckled. "No kidding. But it's best to see the end right at the beginning with these internet dates."

She took another bite of her hot dog and chewed. He did the same, suspecting there'd be a change of topic when she swallowed.

"How cute is my Jack?"

And there it was. A much safer subject. "He's a hoot. Fat, happy, and those tiny teeth look perfect. He'll let go of the chairs and tables soon and take off walking any day now." The little guy had come straight for him, and Nick's heart had melted as he'd let Jack hold his fingers to steady himself. "It was great to see a baby in the family again."

She blinked. "You're Blair and Ben's grandad but not Jack's. I'm glad you liked him."

"On sight. And to put your mind at ease, I know about how Jon met Trix when she was already expecting. I can also tell you how happy he is to have another son. I figure that gives me grampa status." He hesitated. "If that's okay with you, I mean."

"It's fine, baby love should be shared. Jon and Trix's story is not a secret, but it's not the usual thing, either." Her shoulders eased downward and settled. "I guess that means we'll see each other occasionally at family events."

"I hope you've figured out that I'd like to see you more often than that." He didn't like that she immediately cooled when she mentioned their extended family connection. "A big part of the reason I moved to Dickens is to be closer to Ben, Blair, and Jon. Trix and Jack are a bonus.

A great one. I never expected to have another baby in my life. And meeting you again...well." He put on his most beguiling expression. "My wife used to say she couldn't say no to me when I looked like this." He waggled his brows.

A burst of laughter proved him right. They were well-matched, with a lot in common. Now, what he had to do was convince Laurel.

"How is it that you haven't met Trix until today? They've been married for months."

"I had to wrap my head around it. When Melody passed away, Jon was broken for a lot of years, but he kept going for the kids' sakes. Losing our daughter devastated my wife and when she got sick, she didn't see much reason to fight. It's true what they say about the will to live."

"Oh, Nick. I'm sorry."

She'd heard most of this on the night they'd met, but since they'd agreed that night never happened, he figured he could repeat himself.

"In a way, I couldn't blame her for giving up. Losing a child should never happen. The whole world feels broken. But out of the blue, Blair told me about Trix and how much she liked her. Ben did, too. Eventually, Jon's new marriage made me rethink my own life. I decided I didn't want to spend the rest of my years alone." He hadn't been ready to give up. And look at the miracles that had come his way since. "Jon and I spoke on the phone, of course, but I didn't want to push my way into his new marriage. Then, when I called to talk to him about moving here, he sounded enthusiastic. I took him at his word that Trix would love a grampa in Jack's life."

He took heart when Laurel nodded in understanding. "Trix doesn't remember much about her dad. Keith loved her to bits, though. We decided it was time to have another child but before we could, I lost him." Again, she looked toward a place he couldn't see, and he let her commune with her memories. "He'd have been the best grandad."

After a moment, she came back to him with a sheen in her eyes. "But you'll make a wonderful grampa."

He repeated what he said the first time he'd heard this. "I'm sorry you didn't have more time with Keith. You both deserved a full life together."

"Thanks. We did." She frowned. "At least you started dating, but I only tried once and gave up. When Trix was in kindergarten, I dated the mayor. He was nice, but there wasn't a spark for either of us. And he didn't take to Trix the way I'd expect. People said to give it time, but...." She shrugged. "I put her first."

He nodded. "Most women my age have families. Grandkids. In-laws. When Jeanie got sick, I rarely saw Blair and Ben. I suspect Jon didn't want to intrude on our grief and worry. Now, I want to make up for lost time. Retirement in Florida sounds like a good idea, but it takes you away from the ones you love the most." Phone calls and video chats weren't cutting it anymore. "Blair and Ben are driving now, and college isn't far away. If I hadn't moved to Dickens, it might be years before I set eyes on them again."

He had more to say, but he wanted to move forward, not rehash a past that didn't help win her over.

"They're wonderful kids," she was saying. "Blair is incredibly talented at woodworking. People come from all over the state to buy her game boards and to watch her make them at her booth."

"She tells me she's busy enough to set up a website and sell that way now, too." He'd had no idea she was handy with tools, because she'd been shy about sharing her interest. Now that he lived here, he didn't have to miss the next great thing in her life. "And Jon's teaching Ben a few things about cars. They're restoring one for him to take to college."

She nodded in agreement. "People complain about teenagers, but Jon has raised them well."

He sipped his cooling hot chocolate. "Melody would be proud of them. And happy, too, that Jon found Trix."

"I hope so because I'm glad he's in her life. And that you'll be in Jack's." Her earnest expression backed up her words.

"I'm glad, too. Life has a funny way of working out." He said nothing about how surprised and happy he felt about her living in Dickens. Moving too quickly could jinx him.

AFTER LUNCH AND WHEN Nick had gone, Laurel finished her rounds talking with the vendors about their plans for the Christmas rush. Sales had already picked up for the season and newer vendors needed coaching as to what to expect. She went to report to Trix that everyone was onboard with their decorating scheme. Booths would keep things simple while the major display would be in the center of the open space.

"Hi," she began when she reached the office at the top of the stairs. Her daughter had just changed the baby and Laurel had a few minutes to cuddle Jack before he fell into slumber. Luckily, his naptimes were predictable. But that would change soon as he grew into needing only one nap a day.

"Blair's finished with her project for the Christmas display," she reported. "The red ladder is about eight feet tall, and she decided to have three elves on it decorating the tree. One looks like he's hanging tinsel, the other an ornament and the last is placing a string of popcorn."

"Amazing. She's incredibly talented." Trix settled the sleepy Jack in his play yard. Accustomed to voices in the office while he slept, they didn't need to whisper, but kept their tones modulated so as not to startle him. "But an eight-foot ladder will mean a taller tree."

"She thought of that. The highest elf is at the six-foot mark so the extra two feet can extend past the treetop if needed."

"Super. That's wonderful. She's a real talent. Thoughtful, too. Keeping the elves close to the ground means little children will see everything."

They'd decided that Trix's stepdaughter had superstitions around people seeing her more creative woodwork before completion. She claimed that now she could make a gameboard in her sleep, so she happily chatted with potential customers who watched at her booth. Some people stood for an hour while she worked. The longer they watched, the more likely they were to buy one or two.

Just when Laurel began to hope that they'd keep to business, Trix raised one eyebrow in question. "Nick St. James told me you two met at the diner last week. He's quite curious about you."

"Oh?" Feigning disinterest, Laurel shrugged. She wasn't ready to talk about Nick. But apparently her daughter had no such qualms.

"He's handsome as can be and seems healthy and vital," Trix added in a coaxing tone.

"Next you'll tell me you think he has all his teeth." She puffed out a breath. "We're not ancient you know."

"I'm aware of how young you are, Mom. How lonely, too."

"I am not lonely. How can I be?" Affronted, Laurel rose to leave. It was one thing to have feelings, but another to have them guessed at. She'd never said anything about loneliness to Trix. Not when she was a child and certainly not in recent times.

"Please sit down, I didn't mean anything by that remark. I understand how full your life is now with helping me here and with Jack whenever I need you. But that's not the same as having someone of your own."

She settled back into the chair despite her reservations about where this conversation was headed. Storming out would cause more speculation, not less. Besides, she never stormed anywhere. Drama had never suited her. No. She was too predictable for that.

Nick's offer to forget about their time in the hotel was kind and thoughtful. She'd behaved poorly at the end by sneaking out. And then in Dorrit's last week, she'd made a fool of herself by dropping to the floor behind the counter. She squeezed her fingers into her palms at the memory. She wasn't sure how she deserved another chance, but, for Nick, she'd take it.

"Actually, Nick made no bones about his interest in you. I believe I answered more questions about you than I did about Jack."

"Jack's an open book." She gave her daughter a weak smile. "He eats, poops, and sleeps like a baby." She rolled her eyes. "Nick *is* interested, not that I remember what it's like to have a man truly interested."

Her daughter raised both brows in a classic tell-me-more expression.

"And I'm curious about him, too," she confessed. "He seems nice. Warm. Friendly." Kind, caring and generous. And he was certainly aware of her comfort. When he'd offered her his jacket she'd said no because the gesture felt too intimate. She'd didn't need to be reminded of his scent or his heat. Both were burned into her memory.

"If he asked you out, would you go?"

"Is that a question he asked you? If I'd go?"

"No, it's my question."

"I'm not convinced that I'm ready to go on an actual date." She felt flustered, out of sorts because he hadn't asked for date when they'd been eating hot dogs together. He'd had the perfect opportunity. And after what they'd shared in the hotel room, he couldn't be shy.

"We don't have to date to see each other; not with him living here and our family connection. I'll see him plenty within the family group, don't you think?" Between the holiday events in Dickens and family gatherings, she'd see Nick a lot. Maybe it would be better if they left it at that. He'd probably already come to the same conclusion. After all, he was online dating. From all reports, it was easier for men than women.

"Yes, but family events would put you in the friend zone right away. You could hardly carry on a torrid affair right under our noses, now, could you?"

Laurel blustered. "Torrid affair? I hardly think so," she lied. Torrid was the perfect word for that night in his arms. "Maybe the friend zone would be best," she muttered, totally confused.

Trix shook her head. "That way you'd add to your family, but you'd still be alone," her nosy daughter pointed out.

Laurel shook her head. Keeping her tone soft, she said, "What if things don't work out with him? I'm way out of practice and I'm not interested in having a man in my life." The half-truth rolled off Laurel's tongue. She wasn't interested in just any man, but Nick St. James came with a lot of pluses.

"If it doesn't work out, you'll still have a cordial relationship with Jon's former father-in-law, a man who will be in my life from now on," Trix declared. "At the least, you'll have a friend who loves Jack the way you do. Love for my son will keep things friendly between you. Jack and I like Nick. I'm glad he'll be in our lives."

"I guess." She wasn't convinced. "But I have no experience in having an ex. Not even an ex-boyfriend from high school. I met your father and that was it for me. Widowhood is not the same as having an ex-anything." She waved away any more questions, but one glance told her Trix wasn't finished yet.

"If your relationship fizzles, there'll be no hard feelings." She folded her hands on her desk, as if she wasn't prying into her mother's life. With a nonchalant shrug, Trix went on, "You're both adults. I suppose managing your expectations here is key."

"I don't have any expectations." Except a nagging worry that somehow, she'd blow it with Nick. Look the fool, too. And it would play out in front of family. Look at the weird behavior she'd already displayed. Hiding behind the lunch counter being the weirdest.

A sensible woman didn't share the intimate details of her sexcapades with her grown daughter. Inwardly, she rolled her eyes at her childish thoughts. *Sexcapades.* What middle aged woman had those? *Oh, good grief. Get a grip!*

"Even better. Without expectations you'll be more easygoing." Trix pulled her attention back to the conversation. "For what it's worth," Trix continued, "I liked Nick immediately. There's kindness in his eyes. Also, Jack lit up when he saw him. Nick held out his hands and Jack grabbed onto his fingers and pulled himself up. I thought he might take his first steps with Nick."

"His first steps will come any minute," she murmured. Family milestones would now be shared with Nick St. James. *Huh.* She wasn't sure how she'd feel about that if things soured. For the first time her life, she regretted not having more experience in the love department. If she'd been betrayed by a boyfriend, or cheated on or had some other heartbreak, she'd know what to expect, but in the dating game she was essentially a naïf. Naive in the ways of modern dating.

If she declined a date, Nick would move on right away. He found dates online, and sooner or later, he'd find someone else to bring to family events. How would that be for her? Knowing she'd had a chance with Nick and fear had stopped her? *So wimpy.* She'd never thought of herself as a wimp, not after picking herself up after Keith died. A wimp didn't face her widowed future with ferocious intent, the way she had.

Nick wanted a partner. He'd made that plain. He was braver than her. She'd denied that side of her life, thought she was brave to be alone. Maybe being alone was not what she wanted now. Thinking of a long, lonely future depressed her.

It didn't used to. No, when she had a toddler to raise, she'd been too busy to think of herself and her own needs.

But clearly, when she went to Nick's room and enjoyed their intimacy, her needs had taken over. It wasn't just the sex, the body parts fitting so well she wanted to cry with joy, it was the warmth, affection, and kindness Nick had shown her. And she'd shown him. She'd given so much of herself to him, far more than tab A fitting slot B. She blinked and again, found herself mid-conversation with her daughter.

"Do you think Nick would join us here for decorating?" She asked aloud, startled by her voiced thought.

"Absolutely." Trix's grin reminded Laurel of the times Trix thought she'd gotten away with something. Hm.

"Good. I'll ask him." Oh, she understood she'd been led to this by her daughter, but Trix had her best interests at heart.

Chapter Five

Surprised and delighted by an early morning call from Laurel inviting him to the market to decorate for the holidays, Nick wasted no time saying yes to the evening get-together. Since she'd made the first date, he decided to push his luck. "What do you say to a drive in the country and a nice, quiet lunch somewhere?"

"Today?" She sounded flustered.

"It's a perfect sunny day and the weather report calls for more of the same. It's a shame to waste it."

A pause and then she responded.

"It *is* my day off." He heard a smile in her voice that made his heart thump. *Go easy. Don't push.* His mind yelled at his raised pulse to slow the heck down.

"Great, since you know where the prettiest views are, you navigate."

"Perfect, there's a lovely, covered bridge about twenty miles east of here. A restaurant overlooks the bridge and river. Does that sound good?"

"Great. How soon do you want to leave?"

"Give me an hour. It's about a forty-minute drive so lunch will be perfect. Unless you've got a lead foot?"

"A race through the countryside spoils the cruise and those days are behind me." He chuckled. "We'll catch the last of the autumn splendor if I take my time." Leaves dropped faster daily, and it had been years since he'd seen a true New England display. "See you in an hour."

They said their goodbyes and he hustled into his bathroom to spruce up. He ignored his usual first date clothes and chose something more comfortable, a cable knit sweater and soft corduroy jeans. He also grabbed a denim jacket on the way out the door in case Laurel needed to borrow it.

"I LOVE YOUR CAR," LAUREL said when she saw his Mustang through the condo building entrance doors. He'd buzzed her place on the intercom, and she'd met him in the lobby in less than five minutes. She'd considered asking him to come up to her unit, but the last time they'd been alone together, things had taken a turn she didn't want to repeat. Not yet. Maybe never again now that the stakes were higher.

His cherry red '65 Mustang sat like a chariot in the circular drive, ready to take her to the moon and back. "Did you do the work to restore it? I heard Jon say that you were the inspiration for the restoration he's doing with Ben."

He opened and held the door for her. "I wasn't aware of that. And yes, I did all the work and still maintain it." He looked pleased with her reaction to his pride and joy. "There's a full gas tank and we've got the whole day ahead of us."

"Sounds like heaven. Especially since the market's in high gear for the holiday sales rush and I won't have time after today." She walked around the car to admire it from every angle. An image of movie stars in convertibles popped into her head.

"I have a scarf in my purse if you decide to put the top down," she said with her voice full of suggestion. Excitement thrummed as she saw herself in her jaunty head scarf looking elegant. She hoped Nick would take the hint. A day on the back country roads exploring the state in its autumn glory made her heart sing with anticipation. The thrill she felt had nothing to do with the man behind the wheel of the convertible she told herself. *Liar, liar.*

"A woman who appreciates adventure," he said with an appreciative gaze as he took in her walking boots, snug jeans, and puffy jacket. She hadn't had a man look at her like this since her prime. She loved the feeling. *True true true.*

With a gallant flourish that made her grin, Nick opened the passenger door and held her hand to help her slip into the low bucket seat. She worried she might land with a thump, but no, she managed to sit without falling into the seat. *Small victories.*

"Did you tell your family you were escaping into the countryside with a strange man?"

"You're no longer a stranger, Nick. Not to me and not to our family. Jon, Trix, and your grandchildren are thrilled you're here." Technically she hadn't answered his question. Maybe he wouldn't notice.

"Good to know. Ben called last night and asked me to join them in the garage to work on his car. I'd hoped for an invitation." He mugged a face. "Although, he's working on a Camaro."

"And you're a Ford man, not a Chevy guy."

His chuckle got carried away on the breeze when he folded the top down. Amazingly, her smile grew wider. If she kept this up her cheeks would soon hurt. She slipped her hand into her purse and came up with the folded scarf. The print was a green and gold pattern of leaves that complemented her complexion. By the time he sat behind the steering wheel, she was ready to go.

The rumble of the engine interfered with conversation as he started the car and then pulled away from the curb. She wondered how fast the gossip would take to travel through the building.

"Laurel was on a date," they'd say. Some would ask her questions, while others would conjure whatever story they wanted to believe. She'd have to give vague answers if she wanted privacy. Thank goodness none of the women on that bus trip to the casino had seen her in the hotel bar with Nick. They'd all been glued to the slot machines.

Her simple directions took them through downtown, around the common and to the outskirts of Dickens. Past Holly Hill Farm, the road began to wind as hills and valleys made up the terrain. Perfect for sightseeing amid the spectacular leaves. The car made tracks in the leaf litter as they moved away from town. They entered an area of heavy foliage that hung over the road, inches from touching, like fingers stretched out toward another hand. The leaves scented the air in the unique smell of autumn, and she drew in several deep breaths.

When the lanes narrowed and the twists and turns became sharper, Nick slowed to allow them to enjoy the fresh air and late morning sunshine.

"I haven't gone for a drive just for pleasure in too long," he announced. "Not since I took my Jeanie out a month before she passed."

"I'm sorry. Is this bringing up a sad memory?"

"Not at all. She only went because I loved it. She was more interested in stopping to take photos. She painted, and she used her pictures as inspiration for her landscapes. We'd stop and she'd get a few shots and then get antsy to return home."

"You're saying it's the drive you love. Not the stops?"

"Right."

"Me, too," she admitted. "My husband and I used to drive down the coast and return on an inland route to make the day trip last longer." So long ago. Before Trix had been born. She smiled at the memory, while loving this new one. "I don't imagine I'll ever forget today."

He flashed her a smile that said he agreed. "Interstates have their uses, but leisurely drives aren't among them."

The talk turned to inconsequential things, but soon she saw how much they had in common and how often they shared smiles and humor. It was the same when they'd shared drinks that night, and later with their pillow talk. The memories made her flush with warmth, but she no longer felt embarrassed. Progress, she thought.

When he announced he loved rescue TV shows, she confessed her love of disaster flicks. "I'll tune into the shows you watch to see if they're as cheesy as my movies. I love the cheese."

He burst into laughter. "One-part rescues, one part romance, one part family drama. Sometimes jobs are on the line or careers threatened."

"Sounds great. I'll try whichever show you recommend." She realized she missed watching shows with someone else. Passing the popcorn bowl and sharing the remote control might be nice once in a while.

Dangerous stuff, her head warned while her heart ignored the warning.

THE COVERED BRIDGE was as beautiful as any Nick had seen. Painted a bold red, the green and gold leaves at either end made the structure sublime. The hills in the background made the perfect frame.

"Jeanie would have loved this view," he said as he slowed around the last curve. The river under the bridge moved quickly over boulders worn smooth by eons of running water.

"I haven't been out here in too long," Laurel said reverently. "It's a living postcard."

He drove slowly over the narrow bridge and pulled in to the restaurant parking lot. The building was in the Tudor style with deep window wells, yellowed stucco, and grayed beams of wood in squares across the exterior.

He spied an empty parking spot and pulled in. There were few spots available, and he wondered if they should have called ahead for a reservation.

"I hope we can get a table," Laurel murmured when they stood inside by the hostess stand. She untied her scarf and released her glorious hair.

"You're fine," the hostess assured them as she walked up. "We just had a cancellation. A window table, in fact."

Ten minutes later, with coffees in front of them and menus to peruse, he admired the prettiest view he'd seen today. Laurel, with her hair free of the scarf she'd worn, her deep pink sweater hugging her curves and bringing color to her cheeks.

"You're a picture, Laurel," he blurted. The sun's rays picked up slight red highlights in her hair as she turned her attention from the view to him.

"You don't need to charm me, Nick. But I'm flattered just the same." She looked vaguely flustered, as if she wasn't used to compliments. He'd thought he'd given her plenty in the hotel, but she may not want to remember any of them.

"I only speak the truth as I see it," he said firmly.

"You're too kind. This light must show every line and wrinkle, but it's worth it to be here. Normally, I'd run errands and do chores today. Playing hooky feels great."

"Lines and wrinkles," he scoffed and shook his head. "I'm here worried you'll notice a bald spot that wasn't there last month." He smoothed a hand over his head.

Her throaty chuckle moved him to grin like a kid. After they'd ordered their meals, the talk moved to family, Jack, and their respective futures.

"Where do you see yourself in five years?" He asked.

"Not at the diner," she said. "In a perfect world, I'd be part-time at the market helping Trix until the Christmas rush is over, then I'd be somewhere warm until spring comes back."

"Semi-retired then."

"I suppose that sums it up. Tell me why you gave up Florida sunshine to come here?" She waved a hand to indicate the outdoors. "This is gorgeous, but this part of Autumn is fleeting. The wind will bring snow before we know it."

"Moving to Dickens was the right thing to do." He pondered how to say what he truly felt. "Being a widower in a retirement community was hell. Every day, women showed up with food I didn't want or need. Some even offered to clean the place."

"Too much female attention? How can that be?" She teased. "It sounds like a bachelor's paradise."

"My grief meant that at first, I didn't see the traps. After a while, I understood that if I became involved with a woman there, I'd have been stuck in a shadow of my previous life with Jeanie. I couldn't slip a different woman into place beside me as if Jeanie had never been there."

The teasing light left her eyes as his explanation took root. By the end she nodded and made a move to cover his hand with hers but pulled back before touching him. The aborted motion made him reach for her fingers. She accepted his touch. "I don't want to pressure you," she said softly.

"I don't want to scare you off." He smoothed her hand under his and his heart shifted. He liked the feeling.

She tilted her head and gave it a shake. "I haven't been out with a man like this since Trix began kindergarten, and you've been online dating. You're much more experienced in this millennium than I am." She chuckled. "That night in the hotel was an aberration." She kept her voice soft.

"What night in what hotel? I don't remember one. If I say I don't remember, then it never happened."

She burst into laughter that made her look like a happy bride. Beautiful. Serene. Confident. He fell into her eyes, so bright.

"The dating isn't much fun, to be honest. It's awkward most times, especially when one likes the other, but the feelings don't align, or the interests are too far apart." He waved his hand to dismiss the other dates he'd sat through.

He went on. "When Jon found Trix after mourning my daughter for years, I saw that staying in Florida and outrunning determined women made me a fool when there might be another, different woman for me. And I figured out I'd never find her there.

"A couple of years in and being alone held no appeal. I needed a new home, a new life, and a different love." Replicating what he had before would be impossible. "No one could overshadow Jeanie or take her place. How about you? Would you want a man just like your husband?"

"I've never thought of a new man, to be honest. When my husband died, I had Trix to consider. She was very young and needed me every moment. I just...got on with it. The police arrived at my door before dinnertime and told me he'd been in a fatal car accident on the way home from work. The next morning, Trix needed breakfast just like every other morning. She needed to play, to sing along with her favorite TV show, to be three. She needed me to keep her life moving forward in the same way it always had."

"You dated when she was in kindergarten?"

"For a couple of weeks. The mayor was a nice man and deserved more than I was prepared to give him. He said he wanted to meet Trix, be part of her life. But when I took him home to meet her, I could see a three-year-old was busier and demanded more attention than he expected. I decided I needed to end things right away or I'd end up hurting her, too. I let him go and he seemed relieved. Today, he's happily married with three great kids he wouldn't have had with me."

He nodded. His own experience had been completely different. He and Jeanie had had a good life together until Melody got sick and they lost her. Jeanie had been so devastated; he'd been at a loss how to help her while dealing with his own heart-deadening grief.

"You're not looking to replace Jeanie but to find someone different. Someone compatible?"

"I'd like that, yes." A partner to spend his remaining years with. He'd found his second love a few weeks ago in a hotel bar, but she'd run for the hills if he said so.

THE REST OF THE AFTERNOON became a lovely blur as they finished a delicious lunch and lingered over hot chocolate, sharing stories of their child-rearing days and their happy anticipation of Jack's development.

On the way home, the shadows lengthened and cooled the air. Nick pulled over to put up the top on the Mustang. After that, it was easier to continue their convivial conversations as their words looped and spun and their eyes glowed with shared warmth.

"Nick," she said as he pulled into the driveway at the condo. "This was a wonderful way to spend today. I can't thank you enough for inviting me."

He drove around the circular drive and parked behind a large passenger van. Neighbors she knew, and some she didn't, milled around to chat and say their farewells.

Until they got a look at the car and its occupants. Then they stood, eyes sharp, tongues suddenly still as they watched the car.

"Oh, great. They must be back from their gambling excursion. They'll have a million questions and if I don't answer them, they'll make up their own stories, each more outlandish than the last."

He chuckled, took her hand in his, and then turned in his seat to face her. "We could start a make-out session and shock them into silence. They'll forget about asking you anything. Trust me."

Laughter burbled up and she bent her head and covered her face with her hands to help control herself.

"I'm serious," he said, deadpan.

"Oh, Nick, you're killing me." She swiped tears away from under her eyes.

"I'd rather kiss you, but instead I'll open your door for you."

"Okay." On the way home she'd fantasized about kissing him in a friendly goodbye. Or giving him a chaste kiss on the cheek in thanks. Or grabbing him by the collar and landing a big smacker on his inviting mouth. Or all of the above.

But now? She decided to let Nick choose.

"I guess this means no kiss goodbye," he muttered. "I understand how quickly gossip moves in a closed community." He gazed apologetically at her.

She nodded. "I've got lots of experience deflecting questions. I do it a lot at work when I don't have time to chat." She kept one eye on the interested residents. Caryn Ellis waved and gave her a thumbs up and a wide grin. She waved back.

"It's already started. Prepare for the onslaught," he said.

"Caryn's a friend and she can deflect as well as I can. She can keep a secret, too." Her friend would understand her reluctance to talk and leave her be until such time as she wanted to share. If she ever did. "Thank you very much for the drive and the delicious lunch. I enjoyed the whole afternoon. I'll see you tonight at the decorating party?"

"Bet on it." He climbed out and dashed around the car to open her door. He gave the curious women a jaunty wave as she awkwardly patted his arm in goodbye.

All the while, her lips tingled and reminded her how much she'd miss that big smacker she'd imagined.

Had her lips tingled on her first date with her husband? That long-ago detail was hard to recall. But they hadn't had an audience when they'd returned home and had taken full advantage of the shadows on her parents' front porch.

The memories of both first dates brought a smile to her lips.

Chapter Six

D *ickens Art Studio and Market*
Compatibility seemed a reasonable ask in a life partner, thought Laurel. But at the same time, it could be considered dull. Did Nick St. James want a daily routine? Lunch at noon, a dinner menu set out by day of the week? Monday for leftovers, Tuesday Italian, Wednesday pork chops? Laurel shuddered at the thought.

She'd had enough routine to last a lifetime. Baby Jack's arrival meant her old routines had been blown apart and she loved that about her life now. She loved the variety that the baby had brought with him.

If not for Trix's pregnancy, her daughter wouldn't have moved home to Dickens. Laurel wouldn't be her assistant at the market. She wouldn't have the fun of babysitting when Trix and Jon needed a break. She even had a crib and toys set up in her spare room for the scamp.

For sure she wouldn't have dropped her dishwater-dull mall walking group or her cross-stitch projects. There were only so many pastoral scenes a woman could recreate without going stark raving mad.

Breaking her old routines had meant she'd taken that fateful bus trip to the casino hotel where she'd met Nick. Bored with the slots, she'd left the other women to their gambling. If she'd known that elevator ride to the lobby would bring Nick into her life, she'd have—what?—chickened out? Maybe.

Even if she hadn't met Nick that night, she'd still know him now. As if they'd been meant to meet.

Fate. The universe. Dickens Christmas magic. Whatever the cause, here they were.

The barn was a hive of activity and Laurel loved her part in it. Acting as liaison between the vendors and Trix utilized her talents to their limits. Some of the artists were easy to deal with while others acted like opera prima donnas. Laurel took care of both reasonable and unreasonable requests to give her daughter time to paint and explore her own art.

Managing people's requests with a smile was one of her best talents. Trix said she had a knack for anticipating problems and finding solutions before a minor situation became a full-blown disaster. The idea made her grin as she surveyed the work that had already been completed in the barn.

The decorations had been hauled out of storage and Jon and Ben had assembled three artificial trees of varied heights in the barn's center square. Father and son made a great team, and she was thrilled they were in her life. She'd come to care deeply for Jon and his children.

How would they feel if one day she and Nick were an item and the next they'd broken up? If Nick was hurt, they'd hate her.

If she were the one dumped, Nick would feel Trix's disappointment. And that disappointment would certainly affect Jon. The domino effect would be impossible to predict or stop.

Laurel and Trix were in the middle of setting up a table for food and drinks for an after party when Nick arrived. He wore jeans, a plaid flannel shirt, and sneakers and he only had eyes for her. Trix smirked when she saw Laurel flush.

Nick grinned. "I'm ready to work." Then he swung a toolbelt around his waist, and Laurel caught her breath. *Oh, my.* The belt emphasized his lack of a belly while making his shoulders wider. *Impossible, but true.* She clasped his shoulders as he'd leaned over her. She'd gripped them hard and held on, stunned at her response to the weight of him, the heat of him, the very scent of him. She blinked but couldn't look away.

"Yes, I see," she managed to say around a breath held. She wondered if he had a great metabolism or worked hard to stay fit. Either way, it worked for her.

"Jon told me the tallest of the trees is ten feet so I figured I should be ready to climb a ladder if needed." His gaze dropped to the table they'd been setting up. "And it looks like you need a hand." He bent, grabbed the table edge, and lifted it upright, saving the women the trouble. She smiled her thanks and silently told her heart to stop hammering.

Her heart ignored her.

"Thanks, Nick," Trix said with a cheeky sidelong glance at her. "We'll feed everyone after the decorating's done. These tables will be full of food soon."

"Sounds great," he said to Trix while gazing at Laurel. Interest and humor lurked in his eyes. She wondered if he realized how charming he could be with nothing but a look. *Of course he did.*

Voices at the door alerted them to the arrival of more helpers and meant the work would soon begin in earnest. Nick turned away, breaking their eye contact and Laurel felt the loss. He commandeered his grandson to help him with the ladder set up.

Foolish. Silly. But fun, so much fun to share these looks and this interest with him. These feelings were fresh and new and at the same time, echoes of what she'd felt as a girl finding love for the first time. Giddy with the wash of emotion, she flushed and when Trix cleared her throat and gave her a side-eye, Laurel huffed.

Despite her reservations about dating him, her heart seemed to have a mind of its own when it came to Nick. This thing could go sideways fast and if it did, it could be sad for the whole family.

As the work progressed, Blair's ladder and elves were a clear hit. Everyone on the decorating crew stopped to watch as Nick worked on the ladder. He placed bulbs with precision in a pattern Trix directed. Laurel's mom oversaw hot drinks, which included mulled cider for the adults and hot chocolate for the teens.

Blair, with her newly acquired driver's licence, disappeared to pick up pizza, roasted chickens and sides for everyone. Ben went along to provide another pair of hands. Laurel had brought enough plates and cutlery for the whole crew. She'd wash the items she'd borrowed from Dorrit's when the evening ended.

Her niece Kayley and her husband, Nathan, helped Nick return empty boxes, ladders, and other equipment to a storage cupboard. Her other niece, Brenna helped Laurel by hauling in a cooler with her husband Jett. In a generous gesture he'd provided champagne for the crowd.

Kayley had a glow about her that hinted of a surprise announcement, but Laurel kept her happy suspicions to herself.

"YOU INVITED ANYONE to the tree lighting, Nick?" Nathan asked as Nick passed him a toolbox. They were tidying the storage room after the decorations were up.

"Tree lighting?"

Nathan, a newly minted husband, grinned. "If you've got your eye on a lady friend, I'd recommend you take her. It's on Saturday night in the common. Everyone goes."

"You mean the whole town or the whole family?" He tossed a glance across the barn to where Laurel stood with her niece Brenna. "I'll be there. But why the lady friend?"

"Kayley took me and let's just say, it was the start of my new life." The grin on Nathan's face was infectious. This was one happy man.

"Really?" He drew out the word to get Nathan to elaborate.

"That's where we kissed for the first time, right Kayley?" Nathan said as he threw his arm across his wife's shoulders and nuzzled her hair.

"When the lights go on, you kiss the one you're with. I made sure to invite this guy, because then he'd see I was into him." Her light laugh and flush of her cheeks spoke of pure love.

"Good to know, thanks." Nick couldn't wait to get the invitation to the ceremony from Laurel. It would be the equivalent of announcing to the family that they were a couple.

"I WON'T BE ASKING ANYONE to join us for the tree lighting. Why would you ask?" Laurel queried Brenna.

"No reason. I wondered about Nick St. James. I heard from Gram that he took you out today in his—how did she put it? —in his flashy red Mustang."

"Flashy red...? Well, I guess it is. We went for a brief drive around town. He wanted to see where some places were. Like the barbershop, the medical offices, a good dentist. Since I've lived here my whole life, he thought I'd be the best guide." She fudged the truth without a smidgeon of guilt.

She should have warned him that her mother had a lot of friends in the condo building and they needed to come up with a story, but she'd been flustered by his nearness in the car, giddy with enjoyment of his company and conversation. All of that had blown up when she'd seen the passenger van and her avidly interested neighbors gawk.

It wasn't like her to fear facing people, but her feelings for Nick were complicated and no one else's business. She looked from Brenna to Kayley who hung onto Nathan while they chatted with Nick. The sisters were up to something with Nick and her.

Which only cemented her decision not to ask him to the lighting ceremony. It was enough she'd invited him tonight. She should have known the family would pick up on the interest in Nick's gaze. After all, they'd seen three marriages in the last three years. Now, it seemed they'd turned their attention to her, the last single woman in the family.

Well, her mom had been widowed for years, but that was different. She was in her mid-seventies and widowhood became her. She was a true matriarch. And in that role Elizabeth Moore shone. No, that didn't count as single.

Maybe Laurel could be like her mother in twenty years; respected, admired, and loved by the generations to follow.

And happily alone.

"Oh, the food's arrived." She pointed out Ben and Blair as they entered. Both teens had their arms full, and Nick, Kayley and Nathan rushed to help them. "Help me unpack, Brenna. And while we're occupied with that, you can keep your comments about Nick to yourself."

Brenna rolled her eyes. "You're not the big news tonight anyway. I was just making conversation."

It was Laurel's turn to roll her eyes. But she couldn't ask about the hint of big news because the food had to be unpacked and placed for the buffet. The crowd of friends and family were already advancing on the food table.

When everyone had filled their plates and taken their seats at the tables, Jett walked to the cooler he'd brought in and opened the lid. He pulled out two bottles of champagne, then two more to give to Brenna and Kayley.

Nathan produced champagne flutes from a box at his feet.

Her mom leaned in to whisper. "What do you think's going on?"

"I'd say another Moore family announcement, from the looks of this."

"We do tend toward the dramatic when we have news," her mom said dryly.

Laurel had to agree. "We've had a lot of announcements in the last four years. Divorces, marriages, unplanned pregnancies, and the other life stuff that those events come with."

"I'm beginning to think you and I are the only ones with no news to announce," her mother murmured.

"Maybe it's easier having no big changes coming our way."

Elizabeth sighed. "Maybe, but where's the fun in that?"

She'd avoided Nick's gaze and had maneuvered her seat so that there wasn't room for him to sit beside her. He sat at the far end of the table on the other side, between his grandchildren.

A hush fell as forks were set down and heads spun to where Jett stood, grinning like a three-year-old with a big fat secret.

Nathan and Jett quietly and efficiently poured champagne and passed the half-full flutes up and down the table. Brenna and Kayley served the second table. Trix, on Laurel's other side, looked on curiously and gave her mother a shrug.

It seemed no one but the two couples were in on what was about to happen.

Brenna and Kayley moved to stand together with the decorated trees as a backdrop. Christmas had come to Dickens and the market geared up for the rush.

"Three, two, one," said Kayley.

"We're pregnant!" They announced in tandem.

A cheer rose to the rafters, while Laurel felt sorry that Jennifer, their mother, wasn't here to get the announcement. But surely...

The door opened and in walked her sister and brother in-law. Both wore broad smiles and made tracks for their daughters. As they hugged, another loud cheer went up.

Reggie and Jennifer assured everyone that they'd been informed in time to arrange an early visit to be here to share in the happy news.

Jennifer whooped. "We're having a two-baby year!"

Kayley and Brenna turned to Jett and Nathan and hugged them, too. Laughter welled as the news sunk in.

Laurel gave hugs to everyone as soon as she could get to them. When she could manage it, she took her sister aside.

"Jen, I couldn't be happier for you. You'll love being a grandmother." Her sister's eyes glistened with unshed joyous tears.

"I can't get used to the word. Hard to wrap my head around being a gran. Mom makes it look easy and fun."

"She does."

"But grandmothers are supposed to smell of cinnamon and apples and chocolate chip cookies." She mugged a face. "Does this mean I have to learn to bake?"

"Only if you want to," Laurel promised. "Now, come sit with me and I'll get you a plate. You missed the decorating, but you timed your entrance perfectly."

"We waited outside the door until we heard the cheer," her sister confessed. "The girls thought it would be fun."

They hugged again while Reggie accepted a dozen or more back slaps from the men in the room. Eventually, the toasts were completed and the food eaten while the lights on the trees twinkled in merry accompaniment.

When next she looked, Reggie and Nick were deep in conversation. Probably a car discussion. Reggie liked classic pick-up trucks, but she felt sure they'd find common ground. The more her family members liked Nick the more concerned she became that they'd be invested in whatever relationship she and Nick embarked on.

Her conversation with her mom about having no changes in their lives rang through her mind. No fun, indeed. "Everything's backwards," Laurel muttered.

"What do you mean?" Jennifer asked.

Startled that she'd spoken loud enough for her sister to hear, Laurel groaned.

"What's wrong?" Jennifer took her by the elbow, pulled a couple of chairs to the side and sat her down. Then she sat and faced her head on. "Something's off with you. Spill it."

She had to talk to someone, and Jennifer was level headed and as practical as Laurel. "It's Nick St. James, Jon's father-in-law."

"I heard he'd moved here and that he's a great guy. What about him?" She glanced to where her husband still talked with Nick.

Laurel searched for the words she'd need to explain. "We, uh, had a fling you might say."

"When did you find the time? He's lived here less than a month." Jennifer narrowed her gaze at Nick. As they watched, the men moved toward the door. "Does he own that Mustang we saw outside?"

"Yes."

"Reggie had to wipe the drool off his chin when he saw it."

"That's the problem right there. They'll go out to see it, bond, and then Nick will have a new buddy in the family."

"That's not what you want to happen?"

"No." She blew a raspberry. "Yes. Of course I want Nick to make friends with our family. It's just...."

Jen's eyes went wide as she put things together. "Wait. Your fling ended badly? How bad could it be? He seems great."

Laurel hesitated so long, Jennifer prodded her with a finger to her ribs, the way she used to when they were girls.

"Ow, cut that out."

"Tell me, or I'll sneak into your bedroom and do it when you're asleep."

"You would." She sighed deeply. "The fling only lasted a few hours. And it was before he moved to Dickens."

Jen drew in air until her cheeks blew up like a bellows. The air whooshed out in a rush a second later. She lowered her voice. "A few hours isn't a fling, honey, it's a one-night...stand? You didn't." The shock made it clear that her own sister saw her as a predictable, conscientious crone. *Bah!*

Laurel nodded. "The only time in my life. An instant attraction in a hotel while I was on a gambling excursion with a group from my condo. No one knows about it." Except for Nick and he was willing to pretend it never happened. Another kindness.

"Okay. This happened before he moved here." The look Jennifer gave her scorched. But deep in her gaze was a glimmer of admiration. "You're not the perfect *lady* I thought you were." She mimed clutching a string of pearls.

"I guess not." A smile threatened at her sister's humor. "Don't make light of this. I'm in a sticky situation."

"I'm not sure you are. No one has to know about you two meeting before he arrived."

She nodded. "He suggested the same." With a grimace, she went on. "I didn't know it at the time, but he was travelling to Dickens and had stopped for the night. He told me he was moving to a small town to be close to his family. We talked for hours before we...."

After Laurel trailed off, Jennifer waited a beat before speaking.

"Did you make a real connection or was it just sex? Because if it didn't mean anything to either of you, then you can be adults and move on." Her sister leaned in and slipped her arm around Laurel's shoulder for a side hug. "I'll never say a word."

Her feelings must've shown on her face because Jennifer hugged her again. "Unless it did mean more?"

Laurel lifted her face toward the ceiling, squeezed her eyes shut and moaned.

"You tell me everything, right now. There's a lot you're not saying, and I can't help if I'm not told what's going on."

"We've been flirting since he came into Dorrit's last week. He took me for lunch at the Old Bridge Restaurant today where I halfway fell in love with him. I think he likes me a lot, too."

A long silence while her sister digested this news. Laurel watched the play of emotions cross her face. Surprise, happiness, then, the inevitable confusion that mirrored Laurel's own.

"Explain the problem again. You don't want him to make friends in the family. This man who you're halfway in love with? What is your problem, Lolly?"

Oh, boy. Using her childhood nickname meant her older sister was headed into lecture territory. "I don't need bossy you; I need understanding you."

"Then explain, please, so I *can* understand."

"I'm afraid that if I mess up with him, the family will be forced to take sides. Or, at the least, it will be awkward for both of us to be at family events. You understand we'll be expected to share Jack?"

Their mom chose that moment approach them. "Who are you expected to share Jack with?" Her frown proved her confusion. "Do you mean that lovely Nick St. James? I can't imagine why he'd be a problem. Everyone's already embraced him as part of the family."

Her sister leaned in close and whispered. "To be continued." The arch look Jennifer threw her way meant there'd be no escaping further discussion.

Chapter Seven

L aurel answered on the first ring, which Nick took to mean she was happy he called. "Hi, there. I've called to say I had a great time tonight. Thanks for asking me." Jon had mentioned the decorating party, but Nick had hoped that Laurel would invite him. He'd been pumped when she did, convinced he was on the right track with her.

"I noticed you talking to everyone." Her voice came to him, throaty and low. "Did you show your Mustang to my brother-in-law?"

"You know it. He's more into classic pick-ups, but I won't hold that against him."

She chuckled as he hoped she would. She'd kept to the other side of the barn most of the time. To be expected, he guessed, since her family had a lot of catching up to do with the baby announcements and Laurel's sister arriving. It had been a hectic event for her after all. Plus, she was still at the diner running the dishes she'd borrowed through the dishwasher.

"I'm glad you've made friends in the family," she said. "From all accounts, they've decided you're a great guy."

Pleased, he came out with the first thing that popped into his head. "I hope you feel the same way."

She sniffed and he imagined her looking down her nose. "Naturally. I don't go driving through the countryside with just anybody you know. I have my standards."

He guffawed. "I'm glad. It's not like I kick dogs and scare children."

"I should hope not." He heard the smile in her voice and pictured the glow of humor in her eyes.

"There are a lot of names to remember. When everyone's together again, I'll need help." A subtle hint that he wanted her near him during family gatherings.

"I'll let them know to re-introduce themselves. It's only fair."

Okay, she needed a bigger hint. "With Dickens being such a Christmas town, I'm wondering what's next?" He couldn't help angling for an invitation to the tree lighting. Kissing her in public with her family there tempted him.

"The next big thing will be the tree lighting ceremony in the common. Everyone goes. There are carriage rides, a snowman building competition for the kids, and the teens build walls for a snowball fight. The shops stay open for browsers. It's fun."

She stopped short of inviting him, but he saw no reason to quit. A carriage ride for two would be perfect.

"Would you like to go with me?" he asked. "We could grab dinner after. I've heard there's a great Italian place nearby. Or a carriage ride might be fun."

"Antonelli's is on the lake about fifteen minutes from town. And yes, it's wonderful. They bake baguettes and keep them in a basket by the front door. Whenever we go for dinner, we buy one for my mom. She loves them."

He sighed. "Sounds great. But that's not a yes to my invitation, Laurel. Will you go with me to the tree lighting and then out to dinner?" He hated that he couldn't see her face. If she could read his expression, she'd see how much he wanted this.

Maybe it was just as well she couldn't read the yearning that must be emblazoned on his eyeballs. If he could quit feeling like an excited teenager, he would, but Laurel had him in knots.

"Nick, I, um, don't want to arrive at the tree lighting with you. I have mixed feelings about us being obvious in front of the family. It's *our* family now, Nick, not just mine. If we go to the square and we kiss when the lights go on, we'll have admitted something we'll both have to answer for."

"I was that obvious about the kissing tradition?"

Her laughter rolled from her throat into his heart, and he wanted to capture it with his mouth. "You were. Besides, my niece Kayley told me that she and Nathan made sure you knew about it. Which proves my point, in a way."

He got it. "Nothing we do or say in front of your—*our*—family will go unnoticed."

"Right. And how we conduct ourselves and especially how we end up is *our* business. I don't want to be the object of their speculation, as well-meaning as it would be." She sighed, the sound winsome and he thought hard about what she said between the lines.

"They love you, Laurel and want what's best for you. You're lucky to have them."

"Yes, I love them, too. But they really like you, Nick, and if we end up as loosely connected extended family, I don't want anyone playing the blame game or—God forbid—taking sides."

He considered telling her he had every intention of ending up as a couple, but it was clearly too soon for Laurel to feel the same way.

"I understand. I will see you at the tree lighting but will stand on the other side of the group. Will that work?"

"Thanks. I'm sorry I feel reluctant to be more open, but I'm concerned for everyone's best interest."

"Of course. I get it. We go slowly and keep quiet for now. How about dinner? Any other ideas?" He had to tread carefully and not spook her into quitting before they had a chance.

She hesitated for longer than he liked. "I'll ask everyone where they're headed after the ceremony and if no one else is going to Antonelli's then we're free." She didn't sound certain, but he'd take the maybe she hinted at.

"Great. We'll drive separately and meet there." He cleared his throat. "There's only one problem."

"Oh?"

"The ceremony is still over a week away. I'd like to fill some of our evenings between now and then."

WEDNESDAY...

The action flick got out at nine p.m. and Laurel let Nick walk her to her car. Maybe it had been foolish to ask him to meet her in the parking lot, but she wasn't about to let the gossips in her condo see her leave with Nick. They'd watch for them to return. The news would get back to her mother before Laurel could press the elevator call button.

When Nick had said he wanted to fill some evenings before the tree lighting, he'd been dead serious. They'd been out together every night since the weekend. Yesterday, they'd spent the late afternoon on another long drive, talking and not talking, as fit the mood. She loved the easy silences they shared as much as the lively conversation that made her smile.

"It's slick here, sweetheart," Nick said and reached for her hand. "Take careful steps. I don't want you to slip on an icy patch."

Sweetheart. He'd slipped these endearments into their conversations a few times tonight. While she felt a rush of affection every time he did, she worried he might slip up when they were with family. Sweetheart was his go-to and it meant exactly what it sounded like. He was sweet on her and his heart agreed.

Asking a man to quit was like asking rain not to fall in a thunderstorm.

The parking lot had been plowed and de-iced, but she let him have his gallant moment. A quick glance told her the other movie-goers were busy getting to their own cars and not focused on them. She wrapped his arm with hers and snuggled close to his side. The smile in his eyes when he looked down at her was worth the chance they'd be seen.

They chatted about the movie as they strolled arm in arm. A blockbuster with a huge star, who'd had a big fan base twenty years ago. The plot had been standard stuff. The hero had come out of retirement to save a former boss's kidnapped family. She and Nick loved the action and the quick, witty, word play between the aging stars.

"I loved that the hero ended up with his boss's widow at the end," she said. "What did you think?"

"I believe people should grab at love and new happiness however it comes. If that means saving a widow from the bad guys, it's the right thing to do."

Maybe he wanted to save her from loneliness. The idea unsettled her because she wasn't lonely, not really. She had a full life and felt needed.

Mostly. Sometimes. Didn't she?

"D'you think they always liked each other? That he loved her for years before the movie started?" She laughed at the fanciful thought. "I mean, it's just a movie, but good characters can have a life before we meet them, right?"

"I guess. I've never thought of it that way." He pulled them both to a stop and looked at her. "You have a creative mind, Laurel. I never know what you'll say next. And that's one of the things I love about you."

A warm flush started at her neck and moved up to her face. "There are lots of things I love about you, too."

"Good to know," he said, and nodded.

Laurel thrilled at their confessions. She wasn't ready for the big L, but the small ones were great. Maybe that's what a second time around brought. They were past the wild, hot yearnings of youth. But they still wanted the companionship, shared smiles, and memories that came with love.

Maybe she should step away from fear around the sadness of a breakup and enjoy the moments that brought joy.

But she'd had the joys with Keith and the suddenness of losing him still haunted her. More now, it seemed. As if he wanted to warn her not to get carried away.

When they reached her car, Laurel leaned against the side and tugged Nick close for a kiss goodnight. He pressed against her and when their lips met a fire ignited inside. They'd pretended that night in the hotel hadn't happened, except his coaxing lips brought each memory to the fore and washed thoughts of love lost away in a tide she couldn't hold back.

"Oh, Nick. This is... I don't know what it is. But I love how you make me feel," she said against his neck, where his skin felt warm and smelled of aftershave and man. New bristles prickled lightly against her temple, and she reveled in the feel. His aftershave had melded with the scent of his skin, and she allowed herself a moment to rest and let her senses fill with him.

She'd been right in the elevator. Her lips fit perfectly against his neck, and she took full advantage by licking his ear.

He groaned. "You make me feel like a kid again." His tone went husky and dark, and she thrilled to the sound.

Maybe there was still a bit of *wild* and *hot* left for them after all.

His hands moved between their bodies and suddenly, her jacket was unzipped and his open as he leaned close again. His warmth, his hard chest, his lips against her ear as he nibbled her lobe, took her right back to their first kiss in the hotel room. She wrapped her arms around his body under his coat, feeling the strength and breadth of him take her breath away. One of them moaned lightly.

Could have been her.

Could have been him. Either way, she felt glorious and giddy.

The erogenous frustration of kisses in public, with cold air surrounding their heated embrace, made Laurel feel sixteen again. The confirmation of wild and hot made her smile inwardly.

"You are the most romantic kisser, Nick St. James."

"I'm glad you think so. Now, kiss me again."

"One more," she offered on a throaty breath.

Twenty minutes later, after kissing her senseless and making her boneless in his arms, he stepped back. Not finished demolishing her defenses, he swept his thumbs in slow circles across her flushed cheeks. Her eyelids drifted closed, the better to feel the light strokes of his callused thumbs.

Suddenly, his hands were gone. Her eyes popped open to see him walk away.

She touched her lips with fingers that trembled. She wanted— *oh!* — she wanted to call him back, to take him home, to be with him the way they'd been before. By the time she could frame a request he'd reached his car and unlocked the door.

If he looked back, she'd call out to him. She'd make her lungs draw breath, her throat work, and her words form. She'd say the things she knew he wanted to hear.

But he didn't look back. Not once.

Chapter Eight

Walking away from Laurel had been tough, but he held to his decision. Nick climbed into his car and waited for Laurel to back out of her parking spot and leave the cinema's lot. He followed a minute later and reluctantly turned in the opposite direction to head home. He strove to continue in the right direction, because he still had boxes to unpack in the townhouse behind Main Street. His heart wasn't in it because it was the small stuff like mementoes and photos he had left to uncover.

Little things sometimes ambushed him. The memories the photos invoked were bittersweet and swamped him at the strangest moments. Sometimes those moments washed him with pain.

He focused on mundane chores that waited for him, like taking out the garbage and breaking down his empty moving boxes. He'd much rather be with Laurel. Even if she'd cooled off and didn't want him to stay the night, he'd love to share a mug of hot chocolate and a bowl of popcorn in front of her TV.

But his new place would never feel like home if he didn't make it homey. Yesterday, he'd found a box of mementoes from Melody's childhood that Jeanie had kept. He should put a couple of the old pictures on his fridge door. Her childhood softball trophy belonged on the mantel.

Jeanie had laminated a few favorite family holiday photos and put magnets on the back so they could see their happy past whenever they opened the fridge door. When Melody passed away, Jeanie took them down, as if all their happy times hadn't happened.

But they had, and he needed the comfort of those memories if they pained him at first or not.

That, and he wanted to get the feel of Laurel's kisses off his lips. He'd lost his mind when he'd opened their coats and held her close, warm, and inviting, against him. The rush had gone through him, and he'd pressed against her like a fifteen-year-old with his first crush.

When she pressed back, he'd taken things further than he'd planned and by the end, they were both breathing hard.

He shouldn't have rushed her, but she didn't seem to mind. In fact, he'd bet she'd have invited him to spend the night if he'd asked. Walking away was the better choice for his long-term goal.

At this point, another night spent with her would do more harm than good. Her feelings ran hot and cold and with good reason. It was too soon for her. If she felt any pressure to take things to the next level, she'd balk.

Plus, he understood her reluctance to go public. They would have too many eyes on them. Each interaction they had would be scrutinized and discussed among family.

Between a couple who didn't share family, that would be no problem. A breakup would simply mean leaving the family, too. But that option wasn't open to them. He had to step carefully with Laurel because they had years ahead to see each other at family gatherings.

At home a few minutes later, he opened the hand-carved box of memories. The visceral punch to the gut came as expected. He waited a moment, and the pain subsided, driven away by the warmth of the love he remembered. He needed the warmth and with time he expected the agony to soften.

His phone buzzed and when he saw who'd called, he answered immediately. "Ben, hello! What can I do for you?" He checked the time and realized to a teen that calling at ten thirty at night seemed reasonable. Happy to hear from Ben at any hour, he appreciated the call.

"Hi, Grampa. Dad and I need to rebuild the starter motor and he's never done that before. Have you?"

"I have. It's been a few years, but it'll come back to me."

"Great! If you teach me, then I'll never forget how."

He chuckled at the obvious, unnecessary, flattery. "Is tomorrow after school soon enough?"

"Yeah, thanks. We'll see you then."

And just like that, he accepted his family would build more memories. He'd be sure to take a picture or two. Ben with a smudge of grease on his cheek, or his face focused on getting an important part inserted correctly. Either image would look great on the fridge.

He went back to the memory box and picked out a photo of Melody on her first two-wheeler, another of their family on a trip to the Grand Canyon, where Jeanie pretended to fall into the chasm. His smile at her remembered antics filled with the gentle love she gave so freely.

BY DINNERTIME THE NEXT day, Nick figured out what to do to fix the starter.

"We'll get the solenoid switch replaced as soon as we can," Nick explained. "No problem." He suspected Jon had known what part needed replacing but wanted to give him a chance to hang out in the garage with Ben.

Jon had gone into the house after greeting him, leaving grandfather and grandson alone. The two had worked well together as Nick had taught Ben what he knew about starter motors. Conversation had flowed easily, and the boy had touched on girls and dating and his college dreams.

"You're here for dinner, right?" The invitation came as they put away their tools and tidied up.

"If Trix will feed me, I'll eat. But we should check with her first. She may not have planned for company."

"Don't worry, Trix is great," his grandson assured. "She says I have a hollow leg. There's plenty extra for dinner. She's a good cook."

"Well, that's lucky. I'm still learning, but I can microwave a frozen lasagna with the best of them."

"You must miss Gramma, huh." Ben looked at him solemnly and Nick felt struck by how the youngster showed compassion for an old, lonely man. An image of Laurel flashed into his mind, and he acknowledged that he hadn't been lonely since he'd walked into Dorrit's and seen her dive to the floor behind the counter. The memory brought out a grin.

But Ben hadn't asked about his life now, so he replied, "I miss Gramma every day. I hope you find someone who loves you as much as she loved us all."

Ben nodded. "I think it's important to find a girl who can do lots of things. Like cooking and taking care of her family. Like my mom did, and Gramma did."

"Don't tell me you mean to keep a wife in the kitchen all day." If Ben thought women were only good for homemaking he had some serious surprises in store. He wiped his hands on a rag and passed it to Ben. "We'll scrub up in the utility sink in the laundry room."

Ben nodded. "Dad says we need to clean up after ourselves, too. We used to leave cleaning up for the weekend, but now, we're doing that stuff right away. He says it's only fair since Trix has Jack and a business to run, plus her painting."

"Your dad's a smart man. Always was. Imagine how it would have been if he'd never set foot in a kitchen or ever tossed in a load of laundry. When your mom got sick, he already knew how to deal with chores."

"Yeah, it was hard. He worked a lot and when he got home, he took care of us, too. Blair and I tried to help."

"Your Mom told us how much you both pitched in while she was sick." They'd been kids, thrust into responsibilities they shouldn't have had to face. "I'm glad you see the work it takes to run a household. No one should have to do it alone." He hid a smile. Jon was raising his children right. Melody had chosen well, despite the too-young start.

"Before Trix, Blair and I took dad for granted." Ben raised and dropped a shoulder. "I feel kind of bad for not helping more."

"You were a kid, and your parents didn't want you to miss out on being one. Your mom asked your dad to let you kids off the hook, so he did." He patted the boy on the shoulder. "Maybe your grandmother and I should have moved to Dickens. We could've been around more. Helped out." They'd been swallowed by their grief and couldn't see past it. He'd have to live with that regret.

"You're here now and I'm glad we can hang out. I want to learn a lot about cars."

"And I'll teach you everything I've learned. But these days you'll need to understand more about the technology and computer stuff cars have now. I can't help much with that."

"I tell you what, if you buy a new car, I'll teach you how to use the tech. Deal?"

"Even the fancy stuff?"

"Yep."

"Deal."

They put away the rest of their tools and Ben cleared his throat, working himself up to ask something.

"When you met Gramma, how did you know she was the right one?"

He froze for a moment then turned and looked Ben in the eye. "I just knew. I saw something in her eyes, I think. A kindness. She was sweet and had a beautiful smile that I wanted to see every day of my life."

"I've figured out that I want a girl who's nice to everyone."

"Aside from the kitchen duty?" He grinned. Since this conversation had turned suddenly thoughtful, he paused with his hand on the doorknob. He released the knob and faced this half-grown man with deep thoughts who had more to say.

"Yeah. Last week I thought I liked this girl who's pretty and popular."

"I remember the feeling. What changed your mind?"

"Cissie was real mean to another girl just because she wasn't dressed cool enough." Ben grimaced. "I didn't see anything wrong with what she had on, but her eyes went sad. Later, I found Emma by her locker and asked her to go for a walk. She's the nice one, not Cissie. And that made her prettier, too."

"Ben, you learned the most important lesson about women you'll ever learn. Sometimes, they're not as pretty as they look. A man's got to look deeper. That's when you'll see their real beauty."

"I guess. Anyhow, Emma's smart and wants to get a degree in engineering. She needs to figure out what kind of engineering, but she will."

"She's smart, nice, and has goals for herself. That about right?" Nick crossed his arms and ran a hand around his jaw.

"And she smells great." The sigh that came out of his grandson had Nick grinning.

"Maybe you should learn how to cook," Nick suggested. "Because some women are smart enough to look deeper too. Being a partner in the small things that make up a life, makes for a happier marriage." He'd never helped much with the cooking, and laundry, but Jeanie hadn't wanted his help. Today he wanted a full partnership with Laurel.

"I'll ask Trix if she's got time to teach me some of my favorite meals," Ben said with a grin.

"Good idea. And you can teach me whatever you learn. Fair trade for the mechanic lessons." Time to take his own advice. Maybe Laurel didn't want to take on a man who couldn't fend for himself. He should show her he wasn't looking for a maid or cook, but a true partner.

Ben grinned and opened the door to lead the way into the house. "Deal! Maybe you can use your new kitchen skills to make dinner for Trix's mom."

"Why would you say that?"

"I see the way you look at her, Grampa. It's the same way dad looks at Trix. You like her." They walked side by side, Ben confident in what he'd seen and Nick feeling the fool for thinking nobody had noticed. A teenage boy had seen it, and they weren't known for their powers of observation.

Laurel was right. Everyone in the family watched them. But Ben still wasn't finished with his revelations.

"Just so you know, Laurel's nice to everyone, like Emma is. Go ahead and look deep. You'll see what I mean."

"I'll keep that in mind," he murmured.

LAUREL STIRRED THE gravy, watching it start to thicken. Trix didn't like to use packaged sauces or high-salt soups in recipes. She preferred to cook from scratch whenever she could, just as Laurel had taught her.

She heard the back door open and male voices sounded happy and full of laughter. She picked out the sound of one voice she hadn't expected. Nick. Here. For dinner? But with the gravy thickening quickly she couldn't walk away. Instead, she counted breaths until Ben and Nick found her.

She tossed a look at her daughter, busy putting the finishing touches to the table settings in the dining room. She drew her lips into a thin line. "Trix," she said clearly and firmly, "how many are we feeding tonight?"

"Oh, we have an extra because Nick helped Ben with the car after school. A problem with something that Jon couldn't fix."

She knew darned well that Jon could fix anything he set his mind to. Just last week, she'd seen him researching videos on car repair techniques.

This was a set up, plain and simple. She stirred the gravy, silently yelling *thicken up already!*

Maybe she should plead a headache and take off. After all, he'd done a good job of escaping the other night in the parking lot.

She wondered what Trix would say if she told her about the aborted attempt at seduction. She'd wanted everything those amazing kisses had promised, and Nick had left her aching. Worse, he hadn't called her since. No funny short texts saying good morning, either.

She'd been happy to come tonight to get her mind off his sudden, inexplicable disenchantment and now she'd have to share a meal with him and pretend to be friendly.

Bah! All of this proved she was right about having a fling fall apart in front of her family.

The gravy bubbled as she stirred, and she judged it thick enough. *Finally!* She pulled the saucepan off the burner and set it on a trivet.

She weighed her options while she found the gravy boat. Stay and force herself and Nick to pretend they were friendly acquaintances or leave and save them both the awkwardness. Leaving would seem odd and certainly she'd have to answer for that option later, because Trix would see through whatever excuse she gave for ducking out on dinner.

Then suddenly, Nick stood in the kitchen, bringing in the scent of the outdoors and stealing the very air she breathed.

"Nick, hello. I didn't know you were here." She kept her tone breezy while she wiped her hands on her apron.

"I spent some time with Ben in the garage. We've got the problem sorted and soon this one will have his car on the road." He slapped his palm on Ben's shoulder and their expressions showed their family resemblance. She had no doubt Ben got his frame from his grandfather. Nick was square and broad shouldered while Ben's dad was long and lean. Grandfather and grandson looked pleased with themselves and the work they'd done.

"Well, you've come in at the right time. Dinner's almost ready," she said, her conversation light and bland and her eyes squarely on Ben.

Nick's gaze ran up and down her body, taking inventory. She suppressed a shiver of awareness at his warm, interested expression. She could be ruthless with shivers when she wanted to be. She looked straight at him with what she hoped was a quelling expression. How dare he think they'd go back to secret looks and smiles when he'd ignored her for days.

"The meal smells delicious. And looks fantastic." Nick clapped his hands once in appreciation.

She wasn't certain he was only talking about the food. Inside, she quaked that he might find a way to get her alone. She straightened her spine and gave him a dangerous glare.

"Thanks for helping Trix, Aunt Laurel," Ben said.

Nick looked at his grandson. "Aunt?"

Ben nodded. "Blair and I call her that. She's not our real gramma, but she treats us like grandchildren, so we figured...." He trailed off and ducked his head guiltily. She hoped Nick didn't think she'd usurped his wife's place in Ben's heart.

"Well, your gramma would be happy you came up with the idea." He flashed Laurel an unreadable look.

Trix carried Jack into the kitchen and the focus switched to the child as he shrieked with delight at seeing Nick. He reached out his pudgy arms in the gesture that insisted he be handed over. Trix laughingly obliged.

"Here, he's yours while we get dinner on the table," she said to Nick.

"We'll go build some blocks, won't we, Jack. Yes, we will." And the three males sauntered out of the kitchen.

Ben turned back. "I'll help carry stuff. Grampa told me I should learn my way around the kitchen. Might as well start now."

Between Jack, the discussion about the car restoration, and the upcoming dance marathon, direct conversation with Nick was easy to avoid and she took full advantage. She let Trix and Jon explain how the marathon worked with Ben and Blair exclaiming how much fun it was when they managed to make it to the end. Twelve hours long, the marathon went through to morning.

She kept quiet because, like the tree lighting ceremony, it spoke volumes when a couple took to the dance floor. No way did she want anyone to get the idea that she and Nick should pair up for it.

"Aunt Laurel doesn't enter the marathon," Blair said with a cheeky look at Nick.

She put up her hands. "It's enough that I take on teaching some classes beforehand, I don't need to wear myself out on the night of. It takes two days to recover and I'm too busy at this time of year as it is." She shook her head for emphasis.

"Dickens lives up to its reputation," Nick said blandly and lifted his last piece of roast beef to his mouth. He chewed and swallowed, and she sent him a grateful glance. He didn't want to encourage this matchmaking either.

When the meal ended, Jack made it clear he needed to go to bed, so Laurel offered to take him. Anything to avoid more time with Nick. She dawdled and played with the baby longer than it usually took and by the time she returned to the family, Nick had left.

Thank goodness.

She ignored the ridiculous pang of loss that he left before saying goodbye. She needed to get her head on straight and be an adult.

Chapter Nine

She wanted to pretend not to see Nick as he waited in front of her building, but she couldn't. He stood right beside the ramp to the underground parking. His expression said that he wanted to talk. She rolled down her window and slowed to a stop. "I'll be right back," she said.

"I'll come with you," he replied and rounded the car, clearly planning to climb in with her. She could leave the door locked, but that would be rude. Just because he left her hanging the other night didn't mean she should be childish. She'd used up her quota of childish behavior when she'd hidden in the nursery with the baby.

Nick climbed in alongside her and settled in his seat. Cold air surrounded him, and she felt churlish that she'd considered leaving him outside to wait for her.

"Is this your way of getting an invitation up to my place?" She asked, cool and detached. She pinched her lips as she drove down the ramp and through the open garage door. Her spot was only two away on the left. She backed in, shut off the engine, sighed, and looked at him. He hadn't answered her.

The overhead fluorescent lights slashed across his face in geometric angles, as he gathered his thoughts.

"Only if you want to ask me in. I get it if you don't want me upstairs. We'll talk in the car if you'd prefer."

"Five minutes," she offered. If she liked what she heard, she'd ask him up. "That was an obvious set up tonight. Did you know about it?"

He shook his head. "No, I swear. Ben called and asked me to help with his car the other night and when we finished, he asked me to stay for dinner. I'm not sure he knew you were there."

"It's a regular invitation because it's the only week night when everyone can eat together. Ben and Blair are busy most evenings." Nick could've said no to either invitation but his refusal to help with the car was unlikely. And no man living alone could pass on a homecooked meal.

"For sure Trix knew that you'd be invited and would say yes to dinner." She shook her head. "That was definitely a bit of matchmaking. Did you notice how Trix and Jon watched us both closely? They're up to something." Thanks goodness Blair and Ben had been there to carry most of the conversation. Both teens had changed from troubled to chatty in the time since their father remarried. Before that, Jon had struggled to understand his kids.

Nick snorted. "We've been caught glancing at each other. You blush whenever I smile at you. Ben's noticed and when we were alone in the garage, he told me I should learn to cook for you."

He'd noticed her blush. It wasn't as if she could stop the purely feminine response to his interest. Not when the memory of their night together ambushed her at the most inopportune moments.

"Your eyes give you away," she retorted in an attempt to sound huffy and share the blame. But she softened over her next words. "They crinkle at the corners and your smile fills them when you look at me."

He nodded. "Purely biological or physiological response, or whatever it is. I have no control." The steadiness of his gaze warmed her in all the right places.

"Like my blushes." Her tone relaxed as she gazed at him gently. *Oh my.*

They lapsed into silence simply to look their fill. To remember that night, she supposed.

After a warm, comfortable moment, he spoke. "Ben put in a good word for you." He gave her a lazy grin and his voice had turned gravelly. "Told me how nice you are to everyone. I couldn't tell him I already noticed." His fingers moved an errant wave from her cheek and oh, she wanted to lean into his hand. But he dropped it to unwind his scarf from around his neck. The car warmed with both of them in it. The windows steamed up. "But would it be terrible to let them see us together?"

"And if we find we don't suit? I can't live with their happy expectations, and it'll be awful to let them down." Not to mention the years ahead, seeing him. Would they set aside all they'd shared?

"How can you say we won't suit after that kiss after the movie?" His eyes filled with memory and his jaw took on a stubborn cant.

Okay, he wanted to go there.

"Why did you leave me to hang and then ignore me?" She demanded.

"I'm sorry." He looked away. "I wanted to call, but I was afraid you'd assume I only want sex. Please understand there's more to this than our physical attraction. At least, that's true for me." His voice sped up, like a kid who had to get it all out at once. "I like you a lot, Laurel and I want to see where this goes, even if it goes nowhere in the end. I felt exactly the same way that night in the casino hotel. With the time we've spent together since, my feelings for you have deepened. When I found you in Dickens, of all places, I couldn't believe my luck." He dropped his gaze to the console between them. "You were the one who ran out before I could tell you how much I wanted to see you again."

Her breath caught as she pondered his words, his body language and tone.

Nick St. John was serious about her. An uncomfortable flutter occupied her belly. She'd been just as overwhelmed as he claimed to be. It had been fear that drove her out of his room.

"But you did tell me. Maybe not with words, but with every touch and caress." He'd been gentle, caring, and concerned for her because it had been decades since the last time she'd been with a man. She blushed as she remembered her simple confession. He'd immediately slowed down, asked her if she wanted to be with him, if she was comfortable, if she had doubts.

She'd wanted his kisses, caresses, and she'd banished her doubts the minute she'd kicked off her shoes in his room.

She hung her head, sighed, and gathered her truth. "I want to feel hopeful. *I do*. But I felt hopeful when I got married and had Trix." She'd wanted another child, and they'd agreed that last morning that it was time to try. Everything she'd hoped for died along with her husband. "But life doesn't guarantee happy endings. No one knows better than we do that life doesn't always work out the way we want."

She hated that her voice had hollowed out at the end.

"That's true. And I'm aware that we have less time ahead of us than we'd like, but ignoring a good thing guarantees the saddest of endings." He echoed her sigh. "Laurel, if we don't try, I'll forever wonder what if. But if we try and fail, we'll know we made the right choice, and we'll be okay with that."

When she didn't reply, she assumed he'd climb out of the car. But he had one more thing to say.

"Imagine if we'd been this hesitant when we met our spouses." His gaze penetrated her heart. "We wouldn't have known the happiness we had at all."

WITH HIS HAND ON THE doorhandle, Nick prepared to leave Laurel where she sat. Her breath dragged in and sounded loud in the stillness of the echoing parking garage.

"Nick, wait. You're right. I'm a coward and I need to change. But I need help."

"Anything, Laurel, just name it."

"Will you escort me to the dance marathon? Everyone will be there. We can let them see us together then." She looked at her lap as she waited. She didn't say that waiting to go public would give them more time to change their minds if they wanted to, but he understood that's what she meant.

"Okay. Yeah, sure. We can do that." He thought fast. "There's only one problem."

"You can't dance?"

He shook his head. "Not well enough to be on display in front of your whole—our—family. The last time I attempted a waltz, it was with Melody at her wedding. Father of the bride duty. I managed, but she had to keep time and basically lead. I remember her happy voice saying one, two, three, four as we did a couple of turns on the dance floor." He grinned at the memory. "It was a small wedding and over quickly."

"You don't have to be Fred Astaire or John Travolta," she joked. "Just my partner for a couple of dances. It's not like we want to try to win. The fun of staying out late is for the teens, anyway."

"And the point is to let everyone know we're a couple." His sappy grin infected her because she suddenly leaned forward and planted a kiss on his mouth that blew his mind. He reciprocated and showed her how much she affected him.

A long moment later, she dragged in a breath. "Right. And think of the fun we can have in the dance studio alone." Her tone turned husky and wanting, and he got his hopes up. Way up.

"More sneaking around?" he asked.

"Naturally. It's fun, right?"

"What I think is that we need to repeat our night at the hotel." He had more than his hopes up. Her sly smile was all the answer he needed.

"I TAKE IT YOU'D BE willing to come upstairs with me?" She did a quick mental inventory of how she'd left her apartment. Sheets were fresh on the bed. She had a new toothbrush in the bathroom vanity out of a two pack she'd recently opened. She drew in a heavy breath and expelled it with her next words. "I have the fixings for a hearty breakfast."

"Your cooking is not what I'm after, Laurel." And he drew her into his arms and showed her how the next few hours would go.

He'd shown her time and again that he had real feelings for her and hers had never truly gone away. She'd liked him tremendously in that casino hotel and had run out on him before admitting it.

In the days since, the embers left from that one night together had turned into a three-alarm blaze. She needed to quit whining about her age and how these feelings were inappropriate. Fear could make a woman miss out on too darn much!

She needed to quit thinking that her family had any say in her relationship with Nick. Either now, when this felt new and fun, or if it ultimately failed. Especially if it failed. This was their business and no one else's.

She needed to be brave and take the second chance life offered. "It's time, Nick, to see where this is going."

His grin made her stomach flip and her heartrate kick into overdrive.

AS SHE WATCHED THE espresso extraction in the morning, her world felt bright and merry. A well-satisfied woman was a happy woman. And she was one happy woman. The next step in the cappuccino process would be loud, but a glance at the clock told her she had no time to waste. Trix needed her at the studio market in an hour.

As expected, the squeal of the milk steaming process woke the man in her bed because her bedroom door opened a crack. His head popped out as he looked for her.

Nick's tousled hair made his smiling face look years younger. He extended one arm through the narrow opening and lifted his thumb before disappearing back into her bedroom, presumably to dress. He'd showered last night.

Correction. They'd showered together last night and then Nick had spooned her in bed. The drone of his deep slumber had sounded foreign, but comforted her, and she'd soon followed him into dreamland.

She grinned to herself and got down another cappuccino mug for him while she hummed her wordless rendition of the Little Drummer Boy.

They'd had a warm and loving repeat of that night in the hotel except this time, no one had run off. If that night had never happened, the chances were good that she'd have invited him up at this point anyway. They'd been seeing each other for weeks now and their feelings had grown with each date.

Her actions had finally caught up to her feelings for him. Feelings that she fully embraced and gave thanks for. From here on her life would change for the better.

And the reason for the change stepped out of her room and into her arms for a morning welcome.

TREE LIGHTING – DICKENS Town Common

As decided, Nick and Laurel arrived at the lighting ceremony separately. Nick asked her again last night if she'd changed her mind. She laughed and said no. But this time, it was more because she wanted to keep their secret to spite their family's blatant matchmaking. Serve them right, she'd said, and he agreed.

It was quite a game to keep the family in the dark, when right under their noses, he and Laurel spent more time together than before. Sooner or later, they'd be caught, but until then, they had a grand time dodging the truth.

In fact, he felt like a kid again and Laurel had confessed the same.

Everyone had a right to a private life and for the time being, they enjoyed their privacy.

Nick had taken to strolls around town when he was alone and had walked to the common most days. Living close to downtown had its advantages. He got to know more shopkeepers, more of the regulars at Dorrit's Diner, and even some of the municipal workers as they went about their tasks. He'd had a great pastrami on rye at Morty's Deli and bought some Christmas decorations from Trim-a-Tree. He'd also found a cute pair of earmuffs shaped like candy canes for Blair in the shop. He wasn't sure she'd wear them for longer than to show him they fit, but maybe they'd become a keepsake when she'd grown up.

Laurel said the earmuffs clashed with his granddaughter's neon-pink hair and half-shaved head, but she might wear them for the shock value. Whatever that meant.

His life in Dickens felt surprisingly, but comfortably full. He hadn't known what to expect after his deciding to move here. He loved Blair and Ben, admired and appreciated their dad, but to be accepted wholeheartedly by Trix and her side of the family amazed him. Jeanie would be happy with the turn of events.

Dickens was a town that welcomed newcomers and embraced the small-town ethics that he appreciated. People here helped their neighbors. Said good morning. Waved as they drove past.

When he pointed out these things to Laurel, she'd been surprised that he'd noted the friendliness. Having never lived away from Dickens, she had no idea how hard it could be to make friends in a new town.

A large crowd had already gathered in the square and he spied familiar faces. Drawing close to the family group, he sidled up to Jett, who stood the farthest away from Laurel. He was immediately treated to a warm slap on the back and a friendly smile. "Nick, good to see you again."

"Jett, thanks. This is where the action is tonight, huh?"

"Might seem hokey but this lighting ceremony sets off the season with a bang. From here on, we'll see more snow, hear more holiday music, see more happy faces, and feel—I don't know how to say this any other way—we'll feel jolly."

"Like Santa?" He grinned at the notion. He hadn't felt the spirit in years, and he doubted he'd feel it now, but for Laurel's sake he'd go through the motions.

"Well, sort of like Santa." Jett scrubbed a hand down his face. "Life seems to slow a bit, people take things easier, have more time for each other." He turned to look directly at Nick. "Crazy, but the rush of Christmas seems less rushed."

"Before I retired, I used to ask for more hours in a day, just to get the work done on time." Life had been hectic back then. Jeanie had wanted him to slow down way before he did. If he'd known how little time he'd have with her, he would have retired earlier.

After losing Melody, he'd worked harder and for longer hours. It had been tough to be at home. He'd needed to bury himself in work while his wife needed him not to. He could admit it now. He'd failed Jeanie at that time.

He'd done everything he could to make it up to her when she got sick. She'd told him he had, and he'd believed her. But they both accepted she wouldn't fight the end. She welcomed it.

Jett nodded thoughtfully at his comment about asking for more time in a day for work. "But in Dickens, it's as if we've been given more time to smell the pine, see the smiles, hear the cheery voices. Sometimes, I swear I hear distant bells. And it begins tonight."

"You've lived here long enough to know." Jett didn't seem like the fanciful type, not with his head for business, but he hadn't talked with him much.

"I've been here for four years now. Best years of my life. I met Brenna, married her, gave a young teen and her mom a hand up, and launched a new research and development company with them. We're prepped for a grand unveiling early next year."

"I hear it's important work. Global environmental change kind of stuff."

The younger man nodded. "We hope so."

"That'll be lucrative." He was impressed with the vision of a better future.

Jett gave him a steady look. "We've decided to provide the technology for free. Any battery manufacturer in the world will be able to use it to extend battery life."

His shock must've shown on his face. Jett's laugh boomed out. Then he sobered. "So far, we've only told the family. Please keep it to yourself until the new year when we plan a news conference. My assistant is working on that now."

"Mouth shut, but I have to say, I'm honored you told me."

"You're family now, Nick. You may be a former father-in-law to Jon, but you're family to us all." Jett leaned in. "It's the best part of this family, they'll accept anyone, even a grouch like me, and give them their best. I'm living proof of that."

He chuckled and went on. "They had no reason to believe I'd be good for Brenna. In fact, at one point, they thought the worst of me. By worst, I mean, the ugliest thing. That didn't last long, though, once the truth came out."

Someday, he'd ask about Brenna and Jett's story, but not yet. Not until he saw how his own story would end with Laurel.

That, and the mayor called for quiet from the podium in the gazebo. Even the children's voices softened as a hush took over the crowd. The high school choir began to sing Rudolph the Rednosed Reindeer and when it came time to hear the chorus, the whole crowd joined in, Nick included. He didn't even stumble over the old lyrics.

He glanced to his right only to find Laurel glancing back. Their gazes locked as they sang, smiling for each other.

His heart swelled with the music and the look of love in his lady's gaze. Did she know how she looked at him? How much of her heart she exposed in her eyes?

Did she want him to join her for that traditional kiss when the lights went on? Or did she even see the way others in the group had taken note of their interest again.

Because Nick had witnessed some elbow jabs between partners in the group. Faces had turned toward Nick and back to Laurel and he understood the truth was out whether Laurel wanted it to be or not.

He didn't have the heart to tell her that her emotions were written on her skin and blazed from her eyes. Anyone within view of them would see their mutual attraction.

Besides, she'd probably get an earful from her mother, daughter, and cousins before the night ended.

The mayor announced that the annual dance marathon would be in the community hall on the Saturday between Christmas and New Year's Eve. The dance came next on the calendar for the Dickens holiday celebrations. Nick's heartrate picked up as he realized his waltz lessons would soon pay off.

The mayor thanked several businesses for their sponsorships and explained where the children would build snowmen for their competition. Amid the cheers and applause, he noticed Laurel's niece Kayley make her way to the gazebo. A man with a shaved head, sporting a rainbow scarf, held her hand in support as they walked up the stairs to the podium.

She, due to her excellent work promoting the town with a year-round tourism campaign, had been chosen with her colleague, to turn on the lights.

"Our award-winning duo of Kayley James-Brent, and Todd Jenkins, head of our tourism bureau will be lighting our tree this year. Please give them a hand in welcome! They have done wonders getting new visitors to our town year-round and our businesses have flourished, thanks to their efforts."

A cheer went up around him as people acknowledged the duo. Kayley and Todd touched the controller together and the tree lit up, sending a golden glow over the crowd. Children's voices rose in a loud *aww* of appreciation, while the adults, true to tradition, kissed the one they were with.

Nick glanced along the row of people toward Laurel and saw her lips pucker toward him. A moment later, the businesses around the square lit up and a cheer arose.

Maybe Jett was right and from here on, he'd feel the spirit he'd missed for too long.

The pucker from Laurel wasn't close to what he wanted, but he'd take it. They'd come a long way, and each day drew them closer to the time when they'd show everyone their commitment.

He could hardly wait.

Chapter Ten

Christmas Dinner – Elizabeth Moore's home

The rush of arrivals for dinner at Mrs. Moore's had Nick in a spin. He and Jeanie had quiet Christmases, because with only one child, there never seemed to be a crowd, even with their parents there.

This morning had been perfect.

He'd risen from bed with Laurel, then made her his special scrambled eggs. She made toast and bacon while Christmas music played softly. They'd both hummed along, to the music and the rhythm of the food prep. Glorious.

Jett had been right about feeling jolly. He couldn't remember a time when he'd smiled as much since the lighting ceremony. The spirit bubbled inside him, making his walk jaunty, his conversations full of joy and the best of life.

Happiness filled his heart as more people arrived. He felt full of life, of bliss, full of the Christmas spirit. Stationed in the hallway behind Elizabeth, he stood ready to help with coats, packages, and food platters.

He'd shown up five minutes before Jon and Trix arrived with baby Jack. The baby had been handed off to Nick immediately and sat happily up in his arms, splooshing his grampa's cheeks and giggling at Nick's wiggly eyebrows.

Blair and Ben had sidled in, arms loaded with gifts. Blair had kissed her grandfather's cheek, and Ben had shaken his hand.

"You're both so grown up. I'm sure you're tired of hearing it, but it's true. Your mom would be proud of you both." Creative and caring, the both of them. His heart swelled with love.

He'd felt this joy more than in any year in recent memory.

He and Laurel had enjoyed a Christmas Eve potluck feast at Jett and Brenna's house. He'd taken a platter of cold cuts that he'd assembled himself. Laurel had been impressed, which, naturally, had been his goal.

While he'd arranged the various meats on the oval tray that Jeanie had used countless times, he'd hummed Silent Night and contentment washed his heart.

Odd, because his mother hummed that same song while she got Christmas dinner together. The comfort of his memory warmed him. Maybe she was pleased that he'd found family again.

They'd also celebrated Jack's first birthday with a huge birthday cake and one fat candle. His heart had overflowed with love at the sight, and he'd barely controlled his urge to reach for Laurel's hand as they watched the little guy smear cake frosting across his chubby cheeks.

The crowd at Elizabeth's grew when the next to arrive walked in. Kayley and Nathan burst through the door in a whirlwind of wrapped boxes and gift bags.

His new friend and truck enthusiast Reggie, ushered in his wife Jennifer, who promptly held out her arms to Jack who happily obliged and dove toward her.

Relieved of his grandson, Nick helped take gifts to set under the tree, and coats to the closet, which had been emptied of everything but hangers to accommodate the influx of outerwear.

Laurel arrived and proceeded to hug Nick and buss his cheek with a friendly, featherlight kiss. Jack got passed again, and Laurel hugged him tight. "You're so big and we're counting today as your first Christmas, since the real first one was spent in the hospital with your mommy."

Christmas had been forever changed with Jack's arrival on Christmas Eve in a converted stable. The town had made a big deal of Jack's arrival too and the event had contributed to the success of the advertising campaign created by Kayley and Todd Jenkins.

Brenna walked in next and drew in a deep breath. "This house smells wonderful. I'm starved."

Jett, who brought up the rear, laughed and said, "She's always hungry. This will be one big baby!"

Reggie called from the living room, "That's my little girl you malign, Jett. Besides, her mother ate like a horse through each pregnancy." At a look from Jennifer, he quickly went on, "But, I have the most beautiful girls in the world!"

The first half hour saw everyone settle in and through a stroke of luck, Nick found himself seated next to Laurel on the sofa.

"Next Christmas, we'll welcome two more babies," he said, feeling swamped by all the people all at once. "D'you think the house will hold us all?"

Jett spoke up. "I've talked it over with Elizabeth and since we had loads of room last night at our place, we've decided to move Christmas dinner there for the foreseeable future."

"We'll have lots of room for play yards and the babies can nap away from the noise."

Kayley, Brenna and Trix nodded. "We won't have our Christmas sleepover here anymore and Gram can enjoy some peace and quiet over the holiday instead of handling the work that company brings."

"Well, Reggie and Jennifer will still visit and feeding Reggie is a chore in itself," Elizabeth teased. "But these are perfect plans for the future," she said as she checked the time on the mantel clock. "Because the holidays will change from now on." She stood, smoothed her hands down her Christmas-red skirt and walked to the front door.

The crowd looked at each other in bafflement. No one seemed to know what was coming, but the doorbell rang, and they heard Elizabeth open the door. "Let me take your coat," she offered the new, unexpected arrival.

With an overcoat draped over her arm, she stepped into the living room. "Everyone," she said, "please meet my dear companion, Tom

Rodgers." She stepped aside and used the last empty hanger in the closet for the man's coat and scarf.

"Companion?" Laurel said under her breath.

Nick leaned in. "That's more than a friend, right?"

She nodded.

"I like the word. Companion. It works for me." He kept his voice low and for her ears only. But Laurel looked laser focused on the man who stood holding a bottle of wine beside her mother.

"Mom?" Laurel and Jennifer said in tandem. Then the sisters rose to greet the newcomer. Tall, with a shock of wavy white hair, Tom Rodgers seemed to stand a bit straighter as he saw the women advance on him. "Lovely to meet you, Mr. Rodgers," Laurel said in a stilted voice. Her back looked stiff, and her shoulders squared as if she wore plate armor.

While he couldn't see her expression, he heard welcome in Jennifer's voice. "Tom, it's a pleasure to meet a friend of our mom's. Merry Christmas."

Everyone else looked around at each other, various expressions of shock in their faces. Silence reigned for a moment as their collective minds grappled with the truth.

Elizabeth Moore had a male companion.

He and Laurel weren't the only new couple in the family. And it seemed to have happened with no one noticing. He was certain he'd have heard a rumor.

"Nice to meet you, Jennifer and Laurel." Tom shook their hands and seemed to know one sister from the other already. Elizabeth had prepared him well.

The sisters each hugged their mother and turned to the group seated, mouths slack from surprise. "Now we understand why there's an extra place setting at the table," Laurel said weakly, looking pale and stricken.

Jennifer nodded. "And why there's no booster seat on it for Jack. I'll get the high chair from the basement."

"I'll help," Reggie said as he looked at Jennifer with concern. Long marriages meant verbal communication wasn't always necessary, and Reggie seemed an intuitive husband. Clearly, the man wanted a moment alone to gauge his wife's reaction.

Nick approved and wished he had the same right to comfort a fuming Laurel. It seemed the sisters' feelings about Tom Rodgers were miles apart.

"MOM," LAUREL BEGAN in the kitchen not five minutes after the greetings were over in the living room. "Who is this man to you?" Her stomach churned as she searched her mother's face.

She couldn't believe there had been no whisper of this new man in her mom's life. She glanced at Jennifer, who shrugged.

"My dear companion. Do you need a dictionary?" her mother deadpanned in reply.

"Don't be flip. We're surprised and we have a right to be," Jennifer snapped. "How long have you known him?" she demanded and gave Laurel a sharp elbow to the ribs.

Laurel straightened and gave her sister an elbow back. After the childish display, they both focused on their mom.

"I've known Tom for over fifty years," their mother said blithely as she turned on the oven light to peek at the turkey. "This is browning nicely," she murmured, as if their view of their mother's world hadn't just been turned on its head.

"We were neighbors once," she explained as she rose to her full height. "His wife and I were friends, and he was a good friend to your father. We were a foursome and good neighbors to boot."

That took the wind out of Laurel's next question. She squelched mentioning strangers and Romeos and the way lonely widows were taken advantage of.

"Then why don't I remember him?" she asked instead, genuinely curious. Except, now that she thought about it, she wondered if she did recall a Mr. Rodgers in her childhood. She remembered asking why he didn't look like the man on the TV.

"I don't remember him either." Her sister looked just as curious Laurel, as Jennifer's face turned thoughtful. The younger sister by two years, Jennifer didn't recall living in a different house. She only remembered Dickens.

"As luck would have it," Mom continued, " Tom got a transfer and promotion, and they moved closer to his work in the city. When we learned they were moving away, we decided we needed a bigger house, too. The one we were in didn't have room for our growing family." She gave them a side-eye. "We expected to miss our friends, and were sorry to say goodbye but life happened, and the years went by."

"How long have you been *companions*?" Laurel took her turn.

Their mother faced them squarely. "Not as long as we will be when all is said and done." She crossed her arms over her waist and gave them her patented, "I'll hear no more about it," look.

Jennifer ignored the look at her peril. "Answer the question."

"Tom moved to Dickens a year ago, just after Jack's birth, in fact. We were all involved with weddings, Jack, and Trix's new business." She shrugged. "I didn't mention that we were seeing each other. It took months before we felt anything more than friendship renewed. But now, it's more."

"What do you see for your future? Is he in good health?" Jennifer pushed further than was normal with their mom. They'd assumed they knew every detail of her life, that their *mother* would have no secrets.

"We're both fine. And if you're wondering, we both tested negative for STDs." Her sly expression said she delighted in shocking them.

"MOM!"

Jennifer turned her glare on Laurel. "You live here, how could you miss this?"

"They must have been sneaking around. And I was busy with a new grandson, and two jobs. Trix needed a lot of help a year ago." With her position explained, both women eyed their mother again.

Laurel shifted with a shiver of guilt for her hypocrisy, but it couldn't be helped. Her mind filled with an errant thought. Maybe she'd inherited her sneakiness from her mom.

"Eventually, we concluded that we liked our privacy, and didn't want to answer prying questions."

She pursed her lips as her mother targeted her with a considering look.

"Prying? You think we're prying when our mother's been seeing a strange man on the sly for a year?"

"I understand your shock, but this is *my* life and for the time I have left, I want to enjoy it. And Tom's not a stranger to *me*." She patted her chest. "We plan on some travel, enjoying our freedom, and spending the rest of our lives together." Laurel couldn't fault her mother, after all, she wanted the same things with Nick. Didn't she?

"But for how long?" Laurel demanded. "You're in your mid-seventies. How long before you get sick, or he does, and you end up caregiving or widowed again?" Her chest twinged as her heart clenched. This could be a disaster. And for what? A couple of cruises or a month in a Florida condo? She reached for the back of a kitchen chair and held on tight.

Keith had left for work one morning and never came home again. A quick peck on the lips, a distracted goodbye and he was gone forever.

"Will this family ever get through a holiday without a major announcement?" Jennifer asked and moved in to hug their mom. "I'm sorry I overreacted. Of course, you've known him for years. If you liked his character then, I'm sure we'll like him now. And Dad liked him, too, right?"

"He did. I'm sure he's happy we've found each other after all these years."

Well, Laurel couldn't bless this change in her mom's life. She looked away, determined not to soften as her sister and mother hugged cozily.

Her mom seemed infatuated with the past. She couldn't blame her. There were days where she wanted to pretend Keith was still alive. That they'd been blessed with more children, and she'd lived a conventional, happy life.

Remembering Tom Rodgers and his wife in their youthful friendships was natural. Of course it was. But nostalgia couldn't carry a marriage. Her mom hadn't considered the disaster her life would become if she committed to this seventy-something man. The ludicrous idea should be squelched.

"We've certainly had our share of Christmas surprises," their mother responded to Jennifer's question and stepped out of the hug. "Job losses, moving home, divorce, marriages, and pregnancies fill our minds at this time of year. But everything works out for the best." With that, she lifted the lid on the boiling potatoes and checked them. "Done. Jennifer, drain this pot and get these whipped, please."

Laurel wanted to sag into a chair, but she stayed on her feet. "You're right, Mom. Trix certainly had her share of announcements." Her voice, hollow, showed her distraction. Trix had announced a divorce at Christmas, then a geriatric pregnancy on July Fourth, and had the baby on Christmas Eve. That had been a heck of a year. Her mom was right, though because it all worked out in the end.

"Brenna and Kayley have, too," Jennifer added. "This Christmas, though, it seems to mainly be happy news."

Laurel flashed her sister a sharp glance. She had one more question. "Why didn't you say you were seeing someone?"

Her mom looked her right in the eye. "No one asked. You've assumed I'm past it, or that I'm happy alone." She raised her chin. "News flash, I haven't been happily single for some time. When Tom and I met again, all this time after we were friends, we wanted to enjoy each other's company without expectations. We didn't realize our shared memories and fondness would grow into more."

With that, she strode from the kitchen, leaving Laurel and Jennifer frozen and staring after her.

"I guess she expected *some* opposition," Jennifer said, with an incredulous look at Laurel. "But this is a bit much, Lolly."

She cleared her throat. "You can't seriously believe this is good news for her?"

"You don't seriously believe this is bad news? That she's looking forward to happy times and good memories with a nice man? How can that be bad?"

"But that's not all he is. He's a ticking time bomb. One day, he's full of vim and vigor and they've planned their next adventure and the next, he's dead. Or sick and needs constant care. Do you honestly want Mom to go through that?"

Jennifer stepped close and looked as if she wanted to hug her.

Laurel moved away, held herself stiffly and without compromise.

"Laurel, sweetie, what's this about? You're not seriously opposed to this, are you? Why?"

"No one is promised a happy ending, Jennifer. Sometimes the best we can do is avoid a terrible one."

SOMETHING HAPPENED in the kitchen Nick thought, convinced that whatever had been said, Laurel was in a tailspin. She'd returned from the conversation a different woman. Her sister looked confused, and her mother flustered.

Gone was the warm, open woman he loved. Laurel had been replaced by a cold, angry soul who refused to look his way. He'd been completely shut out. Her shoulders looked stiff, and her spine had turned to steel.

Jennifer kept tossing her looks, but Laurel avoided them as well. Hm. The sisters were on opposite sides of some issue and a sick feeling built in the pit of his stomach.

No one else seemed to have noticed because the dinner conversation had flowed happily around him. The pregnancies were top of mind, as they should be. Jack's development had been bragged on, as it should be. The boy was perfect, after all.

But not even hearing about Jack could make Laurel glance Nick's way. No more shared joy. No more shared attraction. There was nothing left of the Laurel who'd walked into that kitchen. Her mother's news had changed Nick's life, too.

He could do nothing except be himself and hope that was enough to turn things around.

Chapter Eleven

"Has Mom recruited any dance instructors this season?" Laurel asked as she held out her plate for a slice of turkey. She smiled a brittle thanks to Reggie as he carved and served, but he was already focused on the next slice. "Show of hands," she requested for appearances' sake. She didn't care one whit about the dance studio, the upcoming marathon or anything else.

Brenna, Kayley, and Jett raised their hands. Ben, who was often shy, raised his hand to his shoulder. Thank goodness. She was afraid her change of topic wouldn't take, and she may have to engage. This way, she had nothing to add to the conversation, because she'd never tell that she'd been teaching Nick and neither would he.

Another benefit? She wouldn't have to look Nick's way. She couldn't. The choice she'd made in the kitchen had changed her attitude and the sooner he realized it, the better. She'd be able to talk to him in a day or two to explain herself, but there would be no going back.

She'd waffled throughout this relationship, nursed her doubts and been talked out of them but not this time.

They were through.

They had to be. She couldn't face another loss. Wouldn't face another loss.

Sometimes the only choice was to avoid the terrible end. She'd had her terrible end once. She refused to have another.

"I'm not teaching waltz," Ben explained. "The mayor said if we have couples, they can take turns breaking as the waltzing couples start to leave the floor." His ears took on a telltale red of embarrassment. He wasn't a center of attention type of kid, not in a social setting. "I don't know how long it will take for the people waltzing to get tired."

Her mom gave a full belly laugh. "Waltzing is an excellent aerobic exercise and people who dance can keep going for hours, Ben. You watch us."

The adults at the table nodded and chimed in with various words of support for the dancers in the family.

"Waltzing couples sounds like code for older folks," Nick commented after the others quieted. Ben and Blair took the ribbing about the younger generation in stride. Soon, he'd ask her about their next lesson.

She dreaded his question because she couldn't trust herself to tell him in person that they were over. She wasn't strong enough for that. She'd rely on texts to get the message across.

"But won't breaking mean the girls can't be in dresses?" Nathan asked.

"They'll change during a rest period," Blair explained. "At least, that's my plan."

"And who will you partner with?" Her father asked, with his fork halfway to his mouth. He tilted his head down and gave her a look.

"We'll see them on Saturday night," Trix interceded for her stepdaughter. "I've met him, Jon. He's a nice kid."

Jon lowered his fork and looked at his wife. "I didn't think we'd go to the marathon. Since everyone else will be there and it will be past Jack's bedtime, we won't have a sitter for him."

"We'll manage," Trix said with good humor. "He can nap in his stroller for a bit."

"Jack will be fine, Dad," Blair said. "You'll see. And I'd like you to meet Jayden there, instead of having him come over and you pestering him with questions."

Reggie cleared his throat loud enough to catch Jon's attention.

"As the father of two beautiful daughters, I may have some thoughts to share."

Jon leaned back and eyed his wife's uncle. "They are?"

Kayley and Brenna rolled their eyes and groused under their breath about life with dad as teens.

When Jon asked the question, Reggie grinned. "Be the house where the kids feel welcome. That way, you'll know the boys who show up and hang out. We had a platoon of boys through our place."

"It got so I started to consider what they liked to eat when I bought groceries!" Jennifer chimed in with a laugh. "But we always knew the girls' friends, boys included."

Ben piped up. "You don't need to worry Dad. I know Jayden and he's a good guy."

Blair's face went crimson. Laurel felt her pain. No one liked being talked about as if they weren't there. She took three deep breaths, held them for a few seconds each, and told herself not to engage. This kind of thing would have Nick glance her way in silent communication. He'd be sympathetic to Blair's embarrassment.

She stared at her plate in self defence. Her shoulders tensed, despite her breathing exercise. Maybe a hot Epsom salts bath would help when she got home.

Nick would be aware of her distress, and he'd want to rub her back, massage her shoulders, run her a bath.

Make her want him in her life.

Oh, she was tempted, but she'd learned when Keith died how painful it was to suddenly be alone. She couldn't go through that again.

Not again. Never again.

The idea that her Mom would one day face losing Tom Rodgers deadened Laurel. How could she go through that grief again? Her mom had lost her dad several years ago and now she wanted to tempt fate. Insane.

"What about you, Laurel? Are you teaching a class or two?" Jennifer wanted to know. She'd like to scream at her sister to be quiet, to talk to someone, anyone, else. But, of course, Laurel wasn't that lucky.

"I have a private student, and we fit in sessions when we can." The truth. She stared straight at her sister to avoid glancing across the table at Nick. "Life's hectic, so it's hit and miss." And it would be miss from here on.

Since everyone was engaged in filling their plates and passing bowls of vegetables, casseroles and two gravy boats, they were distracted and didn't look at her. Everyone except her mother. She didn't miss a thing.

Her mother's pique with her had dissipated like fog in the sun. Instead, she looked concerned and a trifle sad as she took in Laurel's distress.

"Please pass the cranberry sauce," Laurel said to change the topic, managing a brittle smile for her mom. She ignored Nick, but his gaze burned through her.

She should eat. She'd pushed her food around her plate like a stubborn child. If she had her mouth full, no one would expect her to speak again. She stabbed a piece of turkey with her fork. Raised it, but the gravy dripping off the meat reminded her of tears, and she set the fork down again.

Jon looked at Laurel with his eyebrows raised. "Is this Jayden your secret student?"

"Dad!" Blair sounded the teenage girl's plaintive wail.

"No. I'm as curious about him as you are," she said with a small smile for Jon's benefit. Relieved she could move her lips in an upward curve, she shoveled the neglected piece of turkey into her mouth. As expected, the conversation moved away from her, and she didn't have to engage again.

WITH DINNER OVER, NICK wasn't surprised that Laurel pleaded a headache and left right after the gifts were opened. What did surprise and dismay him was her complete avoidance. She hadn't softened one iota.

He had no choice but to talk to Jennifer and ask what had happened in the kitchen. He no longer cared about a secret that had clearly been guessed already.

"Jennifer, walk me to the door, would you?" He asked softly, as he walked past her on the way to deliver his dessert plate to the kitchen. Carrot cake, one of his favorites, had tasted like dust. He couldn't remember eating it.

Jennifer followed with her own empty bowl. She'd had the pudding. Ludicrous to wonder if she'd tasted it.

"Nick." Was that sympathy in her gaze? If he'd read her right, things with Laurel had gone from bad to worse. "Of course. Are you ready to leave now?"

At his nod, she motioned him ahead of her and trailed him out to the front hall. "We'll step outside," she said in a quiet tone.

He slipped his coat on and held his scarf in one hand while she drew on her jacket.

Once outside on the veranda, she spoke. "This is about Laurel if my instincts are correct."

He nodded. "We've become friendly and I'm not sure how to put this, but, suddenly, tonight, she turned into the ice queen. Can you tell me if she mentioned if I've done something wrong that I can fix?"

Jennifer gave her head a quick shake. "Nothing you've done, but she took it hard that our mother's committed to Tom. Her reaction was over the top and totally unlike her. Laurel is an upbeat person, but she went to a *very* dark place *very* quickly. Instead of considering the fun and great memories our mom and Tom will create, she jumped to their health failing, and the inevitable end."

Foreboding filled him. Carefully, he replied. "That doesn't sound like her." Relieved he hadn't done anything himself to bring about this change, he still had no clue what Laurel's reaction meant. "Any idea why she'd go there?"

"When Keith died so suddenly, we were devastated." Jennifer crossed her arms. "Laurel barely found time to care for herself and Trix. She gave up college classes she attended at night, walked away from her friends, focused totally on her daughter's needs." She ran her hand through her hair in frustration. "Laurel didn't give herself time to grieve. She lost more than Keith in one fell swoop. She lost all her dreams."

"It makes sense she'd put her little girl first." Any mother would spend as much time as possible with a toddler if the father was gone.

"Of course. But in some ways, I feel as if the whole family failed her during that time. My daughters needed me, and Reggie and I moved to the city when he got a better job six months after Keith's accident. A couple of months after that, my dad retired, and he and Mom bought an RV and travelled the country. They were gone for a year."

Nick understood. Laurel's support system collapsed and no matter the logical reasons for her family's choices, she suffered each loss.

"She felt alone."

"Nick." Her hand landed on his arm and squeezed. "We all noticed a change in her when you came to Dickens. We hoped that she'd find what she's missed for all these years."

He nodded. "I hoped I'd found a second chance for another happy relationship." He'd hoped for marriage if he had to be honest.

"Give her time to come to terms with my mom's news. You probably don't know this, but Dickens has a way of making things come right at this time of year."

"Everyone feels jollier?" He echoed what Jett had told him, but he had doubts that the spirit would help with this.

"Something like that." She surprised him with a buss to the cheek. "We've never questioned it much, it's just Dickens at Christmas. All manner of good things happen."

"Okaaaay." His doubt clouded his voice.

"Don't give up on Laurel, Nick."

"I don't think I could if I wanted to."

It was Jennifer's turn to look surprised. "This is serious for you."

"I thought she was serious about me, too. It appears I got that wrong."

"Give her time. For what it's worth, I believe you were right about how she feels about you."

He shook his head. "I hope you're right. But she's had decades to work through losing Keith. I understand the terrible shock. He had his whole life ahead of him with her. That's where he should have been; with her. Trix was little and needed her. But, how much more time does she need?" He didn't want to spend his time left alone. He believed Laurel didn't want that either. They'd had a lot to look forward to and she was tearing it away. Out of fear. But it wasn't the first time she let fear win.

Jennifer squeezed his forearm in gentle comfort. "Let Dickens work its magic. She's never responded to anyone the way she has to you. The spirit has something to work with now. It has you."

Chapter Twelve

D*ecember 26th*
A text came in from Laurel at eight fifteen the next morning, their usual time, but Nick grimaced when he saw the message.

"We need to talk," were the worst words a man could read first thing in the morning. He hadn't finished his coffee, and his day had been ruined.

His gut twisted and he pondered the message he should send back. A happy face emoji wouldn't cut it. When he couldn't come up with actual words, he sent two cups of steaming coffee, a smiley face, and a kissing face.

Couldn't hurt.

Besides, he wanted this conversation to happen in person. She'd have to tell him to his face why she'd taken her mother's relationship as a hint to end theirs. He immediately sent another text asking, "Do you have time to get together at three?"

After her shift at Dorrit's, their usual meeting time.

He watched the telltale flashing dots that said she was typing. Seemed to take a long time. Laurel was usually quick on her phone. She took so long he wondered how many words she deleted and changed.

Tension rose as he waited, breath held.

After too long, her response came in the form of a sad face and the simple, but effective words, "Too busy."

For a woman who claimed they had to talk, she did a fine job avoiding him.

The next morning, he got no message, even after he sent his own version of, *we have to talk.*

Fine, he'd go see her at Dorrit's Diner and sit on a stool until her shift ended.

But she wasn't there.

She wasn't at the big red barn, either.

He strolled the whole place, chatted with Blair as she worked her magic on a chess board, but after careful, breezy questions, learned the woman he hunted hadn't been there either.

He had the door open to walk out of the barn when it struck him. Jennifer would've told Trix about their conversation. Of course she would. Jennifer loved her sister and wanted her happy. Trix would want her mother to be happy, too. Ergo, aunt and niece would have talked. They may even have included Elizabeth, the matriarch.

Stood to reason that the cat was out of the bag, and he no longer felt bound by secrecy.

Maybe he could get support from Laurel's daughter and sister and track down his missing lady.

When he reached the wooden staircase that went up to the loft, he hesitated. Laurel might hate him for this, but he had no choice. The longer they went without talking, the less likely it became that they would.

This was new territory for him. He and Jeanie had been on the same page since they first met. They fell in love, wanted to be together, got married. Easy. But they'd been kids, and life had been grand as long as they were together. No grief or baggage to drag along with them. Just their love to see them through the rough patches.

But Laurel had had the same years alone and that was a foreign existence to him, as his happy life was to her. He wanted desperately to understand her and to do that, they'd have to talk.

He couldn't accept that this was over, not without an adult conversation.

Standing at the office door, he waited while Trix ended a phone call. The minute she set her phone on the desktop; he gathered his courage. Trix waved him in, and on sight of him, Jack stood in his play yard with a big wet smile and a giggle of welcome.

"Why does your mother run when she's scared?" he asked without preamble.

Trix's brow furrowed. "I've never known my mother to run from anything."

He took the chair in front of her desk. "She runs from me. And I think I scare her."

"Why?"

He shook his head to clear his thoughts. "Not me, precisely. What we share frightens her."

"Go on." With her interest piqued, her eyes focused clearly on his. Quick as that the tables had turned, and she became the one intent on gaining information. These Moore women were not to be trifled with.

"Your aunt hasn't spoken to you?"

"She left a message to call her, but I've been swamped. I'm curious now so please explain."

He nodded. "Jennifer knows more, but let's just say I met your mom before I moved to Dickens. We had a great conversation, and I had hopes of spending more time with her, but when I, ah, returned from the men's room, she'd left without leaving any contact info.

"Imagine my surprise, when I walked into Dorrit's, and she immediately dropped behind the counter when she saw me. That first day you and I met in this office, was the first time your mom and I talked since we met weeks before."

"You hit it off again, didn't you?" She looked at the ceiling for a moment, then leveled her gaze at him. "She's been busy when I call. She claims she has errands or she's hanging out with friends I don't know. And all along it's been you." She gave him a happy smirk.

He nodded. "The problem is that when your grandmother introduced Tom Rodgers, your mom changed. Like totally. Suddenly, I became persona non grata. She couldn't look at me for the rest of the evening. She left early, too. And that's when I spoke to Jennifer about it."

"I noticed that she went quiet. I put it down to surprise that Gram could hide a new man for a year." She chuckled. "A bit hypocritical when she was hiding you."

"You got it. The sneaking around added to the fun. At least for me." He ran a hand through his hair. "Listen, she's frozen me out. And today, I asked to see her to talk, and she didn't respond. I went looking and she's not at the diner and not here." He scrubbed his hair. "I'm not a stalker, just concerned."

"She's at home, apparently she's got some bug that's going around."

"Right. A bug." He slumped into his chair, defeated. Laurel would never let him into the building. But she couldn't hide forever.

She didn't have to. She just had to wait for him to give up on her. On them.

Trix reached for the phone and called a number. "Hi, Gram, it's Trix. We have a situation with Mom." She listened for a moment. "The *we* is me and Nick."

A KNOCK AT HER DOOR meant it was likely her friend, Caryn. She'd begged off going for their usual early morning walk together, claiming she'd hurt her ankle. She should have used the same fib she'd given Trix about catching a bug. Caryn wouldn't be at her door if she thought Laurel was contagious.

But it wasn't Caryn at the door.

"Nick," she blurted when she saw him. The one person she should talk to and the last person she wanted to see. She steeled herself not to be tempted to fix his obvious hurt.

"How did you get in?" She imagined him sliding his fingers down the column of buttons until someone buzzed the door open. There was always someone waiting for a visitor. At his guilty look she said, "Was it Caryn?"

He gave one brisk nod. "Your mom called her. Do you want to have this conversation in the hall?"

"You told my mother on me?" She swung the door open wider and waved him inside, although telling her mommy should be enough to allow her to slam the door in his face.

"And your daughter. And your sister knows. But Trix is the one who told her you've avoided me for two days."

She groaned. "This is exactly what I didn't want. Everyone knowing, judging, or at the least, taking sides," she said in her frostiest tone. The one she'd perfected at the diner when men thought she made a perfect target for their jokes.

She would not offer to take his coat. Her plan didn't include a long explanation. Standing in front of him, she barred him from moving past the foyer. She barely refrained from clutching her heart, but the rising tattoo must be loud enough to hear outside her chest.

"I'm sorry, but you had me worried." He scrubbed at his head, mussing his hair in that way he had that made her breath catch. "What's happening to us, Laurel. I thought we had this worked out; that we'd show the family about us on Saturday night at the marathon." He smiled, adorably mischievous. "Is it my dancing? Is it that bad?"

She tried to hold his gaze but couldn't because she felt his pain. His eyes were too honest and made her feel needy and weak. "I'm just not interested anymore." She tossed the words out quickly, like darts. "Pursuing a short-term fling in front of our family seems juvenile."

His face turned thunderous. "You're gonna have to explain that one, Laurel, because a juvenile fling is the last thing I thought we were having." He moved his hands, and she stepped out of reach and put up both palms to hold him off. He accepted her limitation and rocked back on his heels.

"There are two problems I see with your statement, sweetheart. The first is there's nothing short-term for me. I'm butting up against sixty and had a long and happy marriage. I'd like to have a similar one with you. Tell me what's juvenile about either of us wanting what we both want. Unless I got my signals crossed with you."

"I just can't do it again, Nick." She wrung her hands, but the gesture showed no clear way to explain. "Everything we'll do in our lives is short-term now. Look at my mother and this Tom. They'll get a couple good years, tops. Then what? Sickness, pain, caregiving. I don't want that for either of them."

"You'd deny them the happiness they could have now?"

He flustered her, made her angry with his refusal to see the truth. To understand the painful loss that faced them both. "Don't make me say this, please."

"Say what? It's over? You don't care for me anymore? Because your *mom* has a man who *cares* for her?"

She closed her eyes as the loss she feared so much washed through her. She'd been an idiot to believe she could avoid it. Her legs wanted to give way with the onslaught. Muscle memory, she supposed, as she fought to control the weakness in her knees. She'd collapsed to the floor on the night when she'd opened her door to two police officers come to tell her that her life as she knew it, was over. She felt the same weakness here, now. And likely forever.

She shook her head. Drew in a weak, wavering breath and spoke barely above a whisper. "It's better this way. You'll come to see it in time."

"In twenty years when we're staring at eighty and we've lost the next twenty to your foolish fear? You're wrong, Laurel. I'll never understand, never agree, never stop loving you." He backed up toward the door, put his hand on the knob to turn it. Before he walked out, he spoke again. "I'll be at the dance marathon, waiting on my partner. If she doesn't show up this year, maybe she'll be there next year. Or the year after that."

"AREN'T YOU AFRAID OF what the future holds, Mom? Because I am," Laurel asked. "Please reconsider giving your all to Tom." They sat in the den, a compact room at the back of the house next to the kitchen. It had been her father's man cave, and she swore she could still smell the scent of his nautical based aftershave. She loved this room with its cozy leather armchairs, one for a guest and one for her dad. The only change she could see since her dad's passing hung on the wall. He'd have loved the flat screen television. The picture was huge compared to what he had.

Her mom reached for her cup of tea that waited on the antique table between the chairs. She sipped. Swallowed. Gave herself time to consider her response.

Laurel would give her the time she needed. No rush. She had days to wait. The rest of her life, in fact.

"I've done a lot of soul-searching about this very thing. What if we only have a couple of years, or months, or God forbid, weeks, before disaster strikes."

"When it comes, because there's no *if*, not anymore," Laurel pointed out. Her mom pursed her lips and glared at her as she set her teacup down. At Laurel's whispered apology, her lips canted into a smile of understanding.

"Then one day, Tom pointed out that while I fretted, I was also letting our good days slip away. I wasted a whole year, Laurel, putting off our plans." She crossed one hand over the other in her lap and relaxed into her chair. "We can't afford to waste another day. That's why we've booked a Caribbean cruise for New Year's Day. We're leaving

Dickens on Sunday morning to spend a couple of days in Miami before we set sail."

"Already?"

"I guess you didn't hear the part where I said I'd foolishly wasted a year." Her mom could be dry sometimes, like now. "But I don't believe this conversation is about me, or Tom."

"You don't?"

"This is about Keith."

"What?!" She'd expected some other man's name to be tossed into the conversation. Nick's. "No! This is about Dad, and you being fooled into believing Tom can take his place."

"If you think I'm taking Tom's wife's place in his heart, think again. No one can take anyone's place, not really. But hearts are bigger than that. They expand if we let them. There's room for more love, different love, *new* love if we're willing to let it in."

"How? That's what I don't understand. How do we move on? Open ourselves to the hurt again?"

"Laurel, sweetheart. We grieve the loss of the first one. Fully grieve. Those stages they talk about are real. Getting through to acceptance can take longer for some. Acceptance is the only thing that can heal our hearts. When that happens, our hearts can grow bigger and get strong again." She rose from her seat and opened her arms. Laurel flowed into them like water. "Please, honey, take it from me, your heart is capable if you give it the room to grow."

SHE'D CRIED IN HER mom's arms for the first time since Keith's accident. She'd forgotten that her mother had appeared at her front door moments after the police left. One of them had asked if Laurel had someone they should call. She'd asked for her mom.

The blanket she'd folded and laid on the ground by Keith's grave was soaked through now. The damp cold ground was unforgiving, but still she knelt there, letting the cold air dry her tears. But she wasn't finished yet.

She had more grief to release, but now, it lightened as she thought of the great things that had happened for her and for Trix.

"She's happy, Keith, our baby girl. It took a long while, but she's happy at last. And she has a son named Johnathan, Jack for short. We never expected her to have a child. She tried for years and had so much heartbreak around those years of disappointment." She swiped at more tears, happier ones now.

"You'd be proud of her. I swear I see you in Jack's lopsided smiles. You never knew this, but you had a way of lifting one side of your lip when something pleased you. Like my pot roast, or Trix's chatter."

Even after she stood and gathered the blanket in her arms, she stayed and talked with him. With Keith, the man she'd given her whole heart to, the father of her beautiful daughter. She reminded him of the plans and dreams they'd shared; of the love they'd had.

Her days had moved along, the years added up and here she was, at fifty-seven, waiting to join him. To be with him again. "You know I'll always love you. Always and forever," she whispered.

Chapter Thirteen

The Dance Marathon – Dickens Community Hall

"What do you mean Laurel's on a break from life?" Nick asked Trix. He already had Jack in his arms, and he had to talk around the boy as he clapped his cheeks and squished them together. He loved every second of it, even if he did sound garbled when his lips were puckered.

His mother gently tugged the boy's hands off Nick's face. "There, now you can talk."

Jennifer leaned in closer. "We were hoping you'd seen her. She called me on Tuesday and said she was feeling under the weather, and she needed to take a break from work at the diner and at the market. No one in the family's seen her since she visited our mom and tried to talk her out of seeing Tom."

"She did?" News to him and it didn't bode well for his hopes for this evening.

Jennifer nodded solemnly. "And after what she said to our mom at Christmas, I'm concerned about her." Jack threw himself toward his great-aunt and she took him out of Nick's arms.

"Has she ever done this kind of thing before?"

Trix and Jennifer shook their heads. "Not even when Trix's dad was killed. She couldn't take the time."

He nodded. He had the whole sorry story, and it broke his heart. Laurel had told him how she'd set aside her grief to take care of Trix. Jennifer had admitted the family had moved on with their lives within months of Keith's death. Not that they should have put things on hold, but it obviously had a profound effect on Laurel. It had caught up to her now.

All her losses, all that grief bottled up. It was no wonder she couldn't face more. Sure, she and Nick were healthy now, but no one was promised tomorrow, let alone years.

The dance had been going strong for an hour and he'd gone through the motions of cheering for his grandchildren and talking to Reggie and Jon about finding a garage where he could work on other cars he'd like to restore. He'd have to keep busy now that he and Laurel were truly over. He'd find a way to accept it. He had to because he planned to live out his life here in Dickens.

Whatever Laurel was doing with this downtime, she needed to do. He was glad now that he'd stayed out of her way this week. She didn't need his love. Didn't want it. She didn't need him hovering or hoping she'd change her mind. To pressure her would be a huge mistake.

She was self-preservation mode, and he couldn't blame her. She'd been through more than most at an early age and the lessons she'd learned then were the lessons she'd live by now.

It didn't feel right to stand here with her family surrounding him, supporting him, when she was the one in need. From here on in, he'd see Blair and Ben and limit the time spent with Laurel's people. It was the least he could do. He'd still see Jack grow up, of course, but he wouldn't share the changes with Laurel. They'd both enjoy him separately.

"I'm calling it a night," he said to no one in particular and turned to find the nearest exit. He'd text his grandchildren when he got home and hear about the marathon from them in the morning. Right now he couldn't muster interest in the outcome.

Behind him the music changed to an up-tempo waltz, which he now recognized as Viennese. He also heard a vague, feminine gasp from the women he'd been talking with. A tap on the shoulder made him stop.

"May I have this dance?"

He turned to see a vision. Laurel. Dressed in a red, sequined dress that skimmed her body like a glove, showing off her curves. Her face shone with hope and joy as she chewed her bottom lip.

"It's a fast waltz and you're very good at them." She cocked an eyebrow and held out her hand, palm up. "I'll let you lead," she teased as if picking up a conversation they'd dropped in absent-minded camaraderie.

"Are you sure you want to do this?" His heart slammed to a halt for two beats in time to the music. When it thudded again, he was certain it leapt with hope.

"As sure as I'm standing here. Nick, please dance with me."

"Am I dreaming? Maybe you're not here at all." Maybe he only wanted her here so badly he'd hallucinated.

But her lips on his felt real, the feel of her hands on his cheeks was real, the way she leaned against him like a woman intent was real. "I'd love to dance," he murmured against her mouth.

When they got to the dance floor, she flowed into his arms, but they barely moved. Other couples swirled around and by them as they clasped each other, needing the comfort of this closeness.

"Why now, Laurel. Where have you been all week? What have you been doing?"

"Grieving. Hard. Deeply." She tilted her head and studied his face. "Nick, I visited Keith every day and filled him in on my life, on Trix's, and on Jack. Before, I rarely went to see him and when I did, I'd shut down so I wouldn't break down. He deserved much better."

He drew her close again. "Yes. And you did, too." He kissed her gently. "I understand about avoiding the pain of visiting. It takes time to come to terms with standing there alone with nothing but your grief."

"I knew you'd understand, even before I did. After spending these days with Keith in my heart and mind, I feel more balanced, healthier than I have since the night he was killed. I'm healed, finally. And because of that, I have room for more love, new love and I want to have yours and more than that, I want to give you mine."

"I'm ready, sweetheart. I'll give you as much love as you need."

"This has been like a miracle. First, we found each other against the odds, just because I got bored at the slots."

"And I was tired of my own company. One look at you and I had to talk to you. The urge seemed powerful, unbreakable. I haven't felt that way since I first set eyes on Jeanie. But now that I've lived here for a while and understand more about Dickens, I believe it really was a miracle."

"I'm glad you talked to me. I never told you this, but the moment you stepped into the elevator, I was eyeing you. I fantasized about how we'd fit together, how my head sat at the right height to nestle into your neck."

With that, he cupped the back of her head and pulled her in. She nibbled his earlobe once and sighed against his neck. "This is where I want to be, Nick. In your arms, for as long as we have. For always."

"I love you, Laurel. You've probably guessed by now that I'd like us to marry, but if you need more time, or never say yes, I'll be here to hold you, keep you, and love you."

NEW YEAR'S EVE – TINY Tim Dance Studio

Tom guided Elizabeth into a turn that made her pretty skirt swirl around her legs and her eyes light with delight. "You're beautiful when you smile like that. I see the girl you were when we met. Although Kate had my heart, you made me believe you saw me as a good guy."

"You were a dear friend, Tom, and a wonderful husband and father. You're dearer now," she replied for his ears only. "Are you packed for the cruise?"

"I followed the list you gave me, if that's what you want to know."

"I'm looking forward to it. We'll have a grand time."

"Speaking of grand times, when will we tell them that we plan to marry onboard?"

"Right before we leave, so we don't have to listen to the complaints for long."

"Complaints? I thought Laurel had got past her concerns?" He dipped her and when she came back up, she laughed in pure joy.

"She is. But they'll be unhappy they weren't included. But a private wedding will be lovely. It'll be enough."

"Yes. It's perfect," he agreed. "We'll tell them to arrange a party for a week after we get home. That'll give my kids time to be here too."

"Perfect. They'll have something to do while we're gone and all of us something fun to look forward to."

"We can tell them about our summer trip to Europe at the party."

Jon and Trix swirled past them and the way they gazed at each other brought joy to Elizabeth's heart. "They're extremely happy together. I'm glad they found each other."

"Brenna and Jett seem besotted." Tom nodded toward the next couple flying past.

"Brenna has never been happier and Jett's like the son I never had. He's caring and sweet, although he wouldn't appreciate hearing it since he has a business reputation to uphold."

Laurel and Nick swept past her mother and Tom, and she made sure to give him her best smile. After another turn, she spoke. "I apologized to Tom, and we had a nice, long talk. He's really a great guy," she told Nick. "He's much like you, in fact."

"Oh ho! How?" he said with a waggle of his brows.

"Fishing for a compliment? Okay, I'll tell you. He's caring and kind and wants to make my mom happy. He treats her the way you treat me; like gold."

"He's smart enough to know that second chances don't come to everyone, and you have to take them while you can, or they'll move on to the next person who needs one."

Kayley and Nathan glided by, happy and so in love it looked like a halo around them.

"My niece almost missed her chance with Nathan. He had some fast talking to do when his wife showed up."

"His *wife*?"

"A youthful mistake quickly remedied. In fact, she's become a friend, and her daughter is important to them, too."

"Another family included in this clan? I never saw how much I missed having people around me who cared until I moved to Dickens. Thank you, for opening up my heart and including me in all these lives."

"It's Dickens. We decided long ago that there's something magical here. It softens hearts, opens minds and brings peace to those who need it."

"I believe this small town is my favorite place on Earth." He nuzzled her ear and sent a thrill down her spine. "And you're my favorite person."

"That's good, because you're mine, too."

"Always."

The End

I hope you loved Second Chance Dance so much that you leave a review! If you do, thank you, thank you, thank you. If you choose your books based on reviews, I hope you'll pay it forward and share your thoughts on **Second Chance Dance**.

If you want to read Jett and Brenna's story you can read: *The Tinsel Tango*[1], likewise, learn about Trix and Jon in *The Rumball Rumba*[2] and find Kayley and Nathan in *The Winterland Waltz*.

---

1.   *https://books2read.com/TheTinselTango*

2.   *https://books2read.com/RumballRumba*

I'd love to see you on my mailing list. For a free introduction to Last Chance Beach in *Hangover Husband*, sign up for *Bonnie's Newsy Bits* on my website.[3]

Writing a review of a book you love is a wonderful way to thank the author and to share your discovery with other readers. If you've ever found a new author because of a review, then please take a moment to pay it forward. A brief note about how you felt as you read the story is all that's needed. I, and hardworking authors everywhere, appreciate every review!

The town of Dickens is home to a wonderful cast of characters and was created for the Christmas season of 2020, in an anthology of short stories. Readers loved the town so much that six authors decided to write longer romances set in the same quintessential New England town.

Four years later and the series has 30 titles and more authors! This year we've produced a FREE cookie recipe book, ***It's a Dickens of a Cookie 2***. Check out our ***FREE*** holiday cookie recipe book here: https://books2read.com/Cookie2

Join our Christmas Comes to Dickens Facebook group for more info on other authors and releases: Christmas Comes to Dickens.

For a full list of the 2024 Dickens Holiday Romance books, please page forward...

3.   https://landing.mailerlite.com/webforms/landing/t6w3o6

2024 Dickens Holiday Romances New Releases

Dickens Holiday of Lights by Judy Kentrus
November 4, 2024
A Chef's Kiss Christmas by Peggy Jaeger
November 11, 2024
Second Chance Dance by Bonnie Edwards
November 18, 2024
The Christmas Canvas by Lori DiAnni
November 25, 2024
Latkes Of Love by Morgan Malone
December 2, 2024
Wrapping Up Christmas by Gracie Guy
December 9, 2024
Call Me Crazy by Kathryn Hills
December 16, 2024
A Dickens Homecoming By Nancy Fraser
December 23, 2024

Other Romances by Bonnie Edwards

Dickens Holiday Romance
The Tinsel Tango
The Rumball Rumba
The Winterland Waltz
Second Chance Dance
Return to Welcome Series
Return to Welcome A Collection
Finding Mercy – Book 1
Loving Logan – Book 2
Craving Jake – Book 3
Claiming Shandy – Book 4
Christmas to the Max (A Return to Welcome Novel)
Love at Christmas
Love at Christmas Collection
Not-So-Blue Christmas
Invitation to Christmas
One Crazy Christmas
Christmas to the Max (A Return to Welcome Novel)

As an author with 40+ titles I can't list them all here! Please check www.bonnieedwards.com for more.

Don't miss out!

Visit the website below and you can sign up to receive emails whenever Bonnie Edwards publishes a new book. There's no charge and no obligation.

https://books2read.com/r/B-A-JXD-HCEBF

Connecting independent readers to independent writers.

Did you love *Second Chance Dance A Dickens Holiday Romance*? Then you should read *Finding Mercy*[1] by Bonnie Edwards!

Seriously? Return to Welcome? She'd rather chew rusty nails...

Mercy Talbot left Welcome on a high—a golden-girl beauty queen who stepped confidently into a bright future. But that was a long time ago and that girl is far, far, away. She's failed in her career, failed in love, failed her family—and she's dead broke.

All Mercy wants is to forget her failures and move forward into a new life with a fresh set of dreams—and get out of Welcome before it sucks her back in for good. But one look at her precocious niece who desperately needs her sends Mercy on a journey into her past that will change everyone's future.

---

1. https://books2read.com/u/4DojzP

2. https://books2read.com/u/4DojzP

Clay Foster used to be Welcome's bad boy, but marriage and his daughter Dilly have transformed him into a devoted father. Widowed now and struggling to be the daddy his child needs, Clay fights his sudden and unexpected attraction to Mercy. But, tempted as he is, Clay can't afford to be taken in by a golden girl. Beautiful, talented women like Mercy always have an exit strategy and when her career beckons, Clay knows she'll leave him and Dilly flat. His daughter has already lost her mother and he won't put his little girl's heart on the line.

In a town full of second chances will Clay believe that Mercy has found there's no place like home?

Also by Bonnie Edwards

Dance of Love
Second Chance Dance A Dickens Holiday Romance
The Tinsel Tango A Dickens Holiday Novella
The Rumball Rumba: A Dickens Holiday Romance
The Winterland Waltz A Dickens Holiday Romance

Last Chance Beach
Make Me
Fake Me
Take Me (and My Kids)

Return to Welcome
Finding Mercy
Loving Logan
Craving Jake Return to Welcome Book 3
Claiming Shandy Return to Welcome Book 4
Christmas to the Max

Tales of Perdition
Perdition House Part 1 An Erotic Saga
Perdition House Part 2 An Erotic Saga
Rock Solid
Rock Solid
Parlor Games
A Breath Taken
The Tales of Perdition A Collection

The Brantons
Body Work
Slow Hand
Whole Lot O' Love
Rayder's Appeal The Brantons Book 4

The Diamond Series
Twinkle, Twinkle Little Thong
Diamond At Heart

Standalone
Long Time Coming
The Stone Heart
The Brantons A Collection
Thigh High

About the Author

Bonnie Edwards has been published by Kensington Books, Harlequin Books, and Carina Press. With over 40 romance titles to her credit, she has been translated into several languages and sold books worldwide. Learn more at https://www.bonnieedwards.com/